BEFORE I LOVE YOU

usa today bestselling author

aj alexander

BEFORE I LOVE YOU by AJ Alexander
www.authorajalexander.com
aj@authorajalexander.com

First Paperback Publication: January 2024
Photo provided by: Cadwallader Photography, LLC
Cover Designer: Wildheart Graphics
Developmental Editing: Made Me Blush Books
Line Editor: The Ryter's Proof Editing Services
First Proofreader: Geeky Girl Author Services
Second Proofreader: Tasha Lewis

dedication

To everyone who's been searching for love.
Never give up hope!
Lightning strikes when and where you least expect it.

content warning

These content notes are made available here so readers can inform themselves if they want to. Some readers might consider these as 'spoilers', particularly for the detailed trigger warnings.

In this case, most of the triggers listed below happen prior to the events in the book, but are discussed in length by the characters throughout the story.

Cheating (secondary character, not on page)
Complications/Death During Childbirth
Death of a Parent(s)
Death of a Loved One
Pregnancy

one

audrey

"Are you doing another reading?" Love asks as she brings another moving box into the living room, placing it next to the front door with the others. "They don't tell you the future, Mom, only what *might* happen."

"You're right, but it makes me feel better." I sigh, shuffling the tarot cards a few times before placing the stack flat on the table and cutting the deck.

I have always been a free spirit. I blame my hippie parents, but I've always been happy. My mom was on the shorter side, barely standing over five feet, and looked exactly as you would imagine. I got my style and short stature from her, choosing to wear flowing tops with floral patterns and skirts that scraped the ground as I walk. Also, unlike my mother, I have warm brown skin, making me the perfect middle ground between my mom's pale freckled face and my dad's, who could best be described as Morris Chestnut with dreadlocks. My father and I had matching light brown eyes that my mother said could see into her soul. No one expected my parents to remain together, but they defied the odds.

Growing up, my mother read tarot cards for a living in New Orleans, and that's how she met my father. They told me the story so many times I have it memorized. My dad was on his way home from the food co-op he ran called the New Orleans Healing Center a few blocks away when he randomly stopped by the store. He had never been in the shop before, but he said he felt compelled to come in that day. For my parents, it was love at first sight. They describe it as feeling like they were struck by lightning, knowing in that instant they were destined to be together. So apparently, fairy tales do exist.

I had a happy childhood, wanting nothing. The love my parents had for me and each other was blinding, but it never wavered. Even when I told them I was pregnant at eighteen. You'd think they would've lost it, but my mom wrapped me in her arms and told me everything was going to be okay. And it was, even if only for a short period.

Love's father, Trey Leblanc, was the quarterback and captain of the football team, making him almost every teenage girl's fantasy. Standing at almost six feet tall by the time he was seventeen years old, I barely came up to his chin. I remember how he'd bend down slightly whenever we talked, putting himself at eye level. I loved staring into his icy blue eyes. My hands would itch with the desire to brush the few strands of his dirty-blond hair from in front of his face. I would lie awake at night, imagining what it would feel like to have his muscular arms wrapped around me as he whispered sweet words into my ear.

To me, Trey was the boy I could never have. Like Leonardo DiCaprio in my favorite movie at the time, *Romeo and Juliet*. He was untouchable, too perfect to even imagine he would be interested in me. Trey was one of the few people who gave me the time of day when everyone else treated me like an outcast, the weird girl whose mom made her eat tofu instead of cheeseburgers like she wanted. I thought he was the love of my life, handing over my virginity to him on a random Friday night. I had planned our entire lives out, but then reality hit.

The following morning at school, he pretended like I never existed. I couldn't understand what was going on until I overheard him and some of his buddies joking around about how easily the weird girl spread her legs. Two months later, I discovered I was pregnant with Love.

At first, I was devastated. Not only was I pregnant and the baby's father wanted nothing to do with me, but all my plans went up in a puff of smoke. I was supposed to be headed to Louisiana State University after graduation to get a degree in environmental studies and work for Greenpeace. I wanted to make the world a better place, just like my parents, but on a larger scale. But when I discovered I was pregnant, my dreams changed. The moment I heard her heartbeat fill the room during my first ultrasound, I was determined to love the tiny person growing inside me. She became my new dream for the future.

After talking to my parents, we decided it was best to tell Trey and his parents about the baby. Since Trey and I had been friends for a while before sleeping together, our parents knew of each other but had never met. I envisioned Trey being just as scared as I was, but both our families would come together to bring this new life into the world. Damn, I was naïve. Trey and his parents called me every vile name they could think of before stating they wanted nothing to do with our child. I left their house with tears streaming down my face, and the papers terminating Trey's parental rights arrived in the mail a few days later. My heart broke for the tiny human growing in my belly, but I was determined to be everything he or she needed in life. To show them the same love and unwavering support that my parents showed me.

Trey continued to avoid me, and I kept my head down, graduated, and went searching for a job. I had been attending classes at the local yoga studio for years and knew the owners. They hired me on the spot. Thankfully I was able to blend in, not alerting anyone else about my pregnancy. Yoga instruction wasn't what I planned for my future, but it came with the flexible schedule I needed to take care of Love.

It was my parents, Love, and me against the world, and I was content with that. We didn't have everything we wanted, but we had everything we needed. Until the unthinkable happened—the accident. My parents were on their way home from one of their many spiritual retreats when a tractor-trailer veered into their lane and hit them head-on. They were both killed instantly. In a matter of minutes, I was alone, barely old enough to take care of myself, let alone an infant.

My parents were never big planners, but thankfully, they left simple instructions on what to do in the event that anything happened to them. But being eighteen and completely alone in the world made me ache for that connection to another human being. Something that I hate to admit still plagues me to this day. Hence, the tarot cards.

"What did you ask them this time?" Love questions, bringing me back to the present as she takes a seat at the table beside me.

"Am I making the right decision to move to Tyson's Creek?" I whisper, my cheeks heating slightly in embarrassment.

This isn't something new for me to be doing. My mom showed me how to read tarot cards when I was fourteen, and it became my passion. I used to do readings for friends and on odd occasions, but nothing too serious. It wasn't until after my parents' deaths that I relied on them heavily. The cards are now a part of me, using them to help guide the path I take through life. Each time I do a card reading, I feel as if she is sitting right here next to me, guiding me toward the right choices. Too bad that I don't always listen to them.

"Mom..." She sighs, placing her hand on top of mine, her eyes full of emotion.

I know that look. That's the look she gives me every time she thinks she's saying something that will hurt my feelings. At fourteen, Love is one of my best friends. She's one of the few people who I tell all my secrets and is always be there for me. But does it also make the line between mother and daughter a little less clear? Yes, it does, but it works for us. People don't understand why I treat Love more like one of my friends instead of a fourteen-year-old girl, and if I'm being honest, I can't pinpoint when it happened. Love and I grew up together, so it's only natural we are close, but sometimes, she is the voice of reason.

"You can't keep doing this. We are making the right decision to leave this place behind. We need a fresh start somewhere where we are both loved and supported."

"I know, honey. But I can't shake this nagging feeling that I'm making the wrong decision. That if we leave here, somehow, it'll ruin everything for you and your future."

Love giggles softly before giving my hand a squeeze. "No matter what you do, at some point, I'm sure I'll blame you for ruining my life, but today is not that day. I'm excited to move closer to Auntie Bristol, especially with my new baby cousin on the way. I can't wait to get all the baby snuggles I want since someone never gave me the little brother I demanded for my tenth birthday."

"See? Ruining your life." I comment as my phone

vibrates on the table beside me, my best friend's beautiful face filling the screen. "Speak of the devil."

"Hello, Auntie Bristol!" Love shouts as I answer the phone. "Please tell my mother that Ian Hudson is an asshole and that moving to be closer to you and my new baby cousin is the best decision for all of us."

"Language," I growl as Love sticks her tongue out at me before disappearing down the hallway toward her room.

"Hey, Bristol."

"You're doing a reading again, aren't you?" she deadpans.

"Yes." I sigh, gearing up for the usual argument between us. "I know you don't understand, but it calms me."

Bristol Reid and I have been friends since right after I found out I was pregnant with Love. Her father was stationed at the military base in New Orleans and rented the house a few blocks down from mine. The moment she laid eyes on me at the bus stop, she decided we would be the best of friends. I swore things would change when we got to school, but they didn't, and I slowly lowered the walls I had up around my heart. I even went as far as confiding in her that I was pregnant. She didn't bat an eyelash. Instead, she wrapped me in her arms and promised to babysit whenever I needed help.

After my parents' deaths, Bristol's family took Love and me into their home, making sure we always felt like a part of the family because, at that point, we were. They gave Love and me a place to call home until I could save enough money to get an apartment and begin living life again.

Although her father transferred to Tennessee shortly after Love's first birthday, Bristol and I have stayed in touch with almost daily video calls. Even though I've moved around a lot since Love turned a year old, Bristol and I have managed to stay in touch. We are as close as two people can be with millions of miles between us. I tell her my deepest, darkest secrets. That's why the moment I discovered what Ian had done, I picked up the phone and called Bristol. I doubt I could have handled any of this without her and the girls' help.

"I don't doubt that, but you can't use a deck of cards to choose your path in life. Making wrong decisions is inevitable; it's one of the things that make us human. The important thing to remember isn't the mistake itself but that we learn from them and grow."

"Look what happened the last time I followed my heart instead of listening to what the universe was telling me."

I've always asked the cards for guidance to help me remain on the right path, but it seems the moment I'm in a relationship, all rational thought goes out the window. I've always followed my heart, completely ignoring the glaringly obvious warning signs staring me right in the face. My relationship with Ian isn't any different. I've been so wrapped up in making him happy, wanting to hold on to him as tightly as I could so he'd never leave me.

But a few weeks ago, I got this nagging feeling something was very wrong in our relationship. I couldn't put my finger on what that was per say, but I sensed Ian was hiding something. He was going on more and more business trips, missing dinner dates because of work, and staying out later and later. When I finally got the courage to ask him what was going on, he apologized, reassuring me that he loved Love and me. He was just busy at work and would make more of an effort to be there for us.

Naturally, I asked the cards if everything was going to work out with Ian and me, but all I got was an unclear answer. This wasn't unusual since tarot reading isn't an exact science, so I followed my heart. Ian loved me, and I loved him. Everything else would work out in the future. However, I couldn't shake the nagging feeling that things were about to change drastically. I thought maybe he was going to propose or tell me he was moving, but man, was I wrong.

"Ian is an asshole, and none of this is your fault," she growls, taking a deep breath. "I refuse to raise my blood pressure for the millionth time talking about this asshole."

"Is everything okay?" All thoughts of Ian and the mess I've gotten Love and me into were quickly forgotten.

"Of course! Now that you're coming to Tyson's Creek, everyone will be in the same place! I can't believe, after all these years, we'll finally be together again. No more celebrating birthdays, having movie nights, or girl dish sessions over video anymore."

"I'm sure Selina and Leia will be thrilled to have me horning in on your weekly gab sessions."

"Shut your mouth right now, Audrey! Selina and Leia love you to pieces and are just as excited as I am to have you here. Honestly, do you think Leia would have offered to let you stay in one of her parents' rental cottages for *free* until you found a place if she didn't want you here? Or that Selina would've offered to give Love dance lessons at a discounted rate until you got back on your feet?"

I know deep down that Selina and Leia never do anything they don't want to, but we're only linked together because of Bristol. We've only ever talked to each other through the computer. What happens if that changes when we are all living in the same place? These three women are the only support Love and I have. There is no one else. If they left us, I don't know what I'd do.

"Thanks for the reminder that people love me, even though I continue to make stupid mistakes."

"What the fuck is going on here?" Ian bellows as he storms into the living room. "Are you going somewhere and forgot to inform me?"

My eyes swing toward the door, locking with Ian's as I sigh loudly. "Speaking of mistakes..."

Ian raises his eyebrow in question but doesn't move a muscle. I continue staring at him, the phone pressed to my ear. "The biggest. Time to end one chapter of my life before moving on to a new one. I'll call you when we are on our way. Love you."

"Love you, too. And don't worry, I have bail money just in case you need it," she replies before ending the call.

Ian drops his briefcase on the breakfast bar before draping his suit jacket over the barstool and leaning his tiny carry-on bag that he packed for a two-week business trip against the wall. Another one of the many warning signs I should've noticed. His green eyes narrow in my direction as he strolls toward the couch across the room. His eyebrows pull down as he looks around and takes a seat, resting his ankle on his knee. He's the picture of ease, as if he doesn't have a care in the world.

I don't say a word, just stare at him as I try to understand what I saw in him in the first place. Ian was charming and made me feel special, something that I hadn't felt in a long time. He was also the exact opposite of any of the men I had dated in the past.

Instead of being muscular and flirtatious, he's lean and introverted. He'd rather spend a quiet evening at home, watching movies, instead of spending a night out on the town. I used to believe it was because he wanted to ensure Love was included in our lives together, but after speaking to his wife, I discovered it was because he was hiding us–his dirty little secret.

Bile collects in my throat as a blanket of shame settles over my shoulder. I should've known what was happening. Should've heeded all the warning signs the universe was giving me, but instead, I chose to bury my head in the sand and believe that love would conquer all. How pathetic.

"Were you planning on telling me you were leaving or were you just going to slip away into the night, never to be heard from again?" he growls out, motioning toward the stack of boxes next to the door.

"I know, Ian," I push up from the table and head toward him. "Your wife called last week, informing me that your 'business trip' was your tenth wedding anniversary."

"Fuck," he groans, his head dropping to the back of the couch. "I was going home to tell her I was filing for divorce, that I had met someone else."

"We've been together for almost two years, Ian. I've been the other woman for two years and had no idea."

Ian scoffs, pushing to his feet. He comes to a stop in front of me, only a few inches separating us. I stare into his eyes, trying to decide if I want to punch him in the face or burst into tears. The smell of the aftershave I bought him for his birthday a few months ago fills my nose as I scan his face. I search his eyes, looking for any sign that he's sorry for what he's done to us, but there's nothing.

"Right. And you were so oblivious."

"What?" I recoil, as if he slapped me in the face. "You did this on purpose?"

"Maybe, maybe not. Look, my wife is a frigid bitch who has done everything in her power to make me miserable. I deserved to be treated well, too."

"*You* deserve?" I screech. Tears pool in my eyes at the irony of this situation. "What about what *I* deserve? What does your wife on the other side of the country deserve?"

Ian runs his hand through his dark hair, making a mess of his perfectly styled hair before rolling his eyes. "You got exactly what you deserved, Audrey, and we both know it. You were so wrapped up in finding someone who loved you that you were dying for a little attention. It was written all over your face the day I met you. At first, I figured I'd give you a little attention and get my dick wet, but you were so oblivious." Ian chuckles softly, shaking his head. "As long as I kept giving you the attention you craved, you'd continue living in your happy little bubble of oblivion, completely clueless to what was happening around you."

He's right. All the signs were there. The long trips to the East Coast, no phone calls, or texts when he was gone. Any rational woman would have suspected something was up, but I saw nothing coming. All I wanted was to find someone to love me. For that all-encompassing love that my parents had with each other. To be loved by another human being with all their heart and soul, as if I were the center of their entire universe. But I ended up being the one to ruin someone else's happiness.

You're trash, Audrey.

You trapped me.

You aren't worthy of love.

You ruin everything you touch.

Trey's voice from all those years ago echoes through my mind as I fight to maintain control of my emotions.

"It was fun while it lasted." Ian plants a kiss on my forehead before heading back toward the door. "I'm going to stay at a friend's tonight. Just make sure you're out of here when I come back in the morning."

"Is this friend a female?"

"Now, is that any of your business?" he says over his shoulder before pulling the door open and closing it tightly behind him.

The tears I've been holding back stream down my face. I wanted to be strong, to tell Ian to go fuck himself and leave with my head held high, but he ripped open every wound I've repaired since I heard from his wife. Most of everything he said was bullshit, his way of trying to make me feel bad for choosing Love and myself over a loveless relationship, but there was also some truth.

Ever since my parents died, I've been searching for love in all the wrong places. Any man that gave me the smallest bit of attention, I jumped in heart first, only to end up heartbroken at the end. Some only wanted a quick roll in the hay, some freaked once I started spouting those dreaded three words, and some lost it the moment I mentioned I was a single mom.

When I met Ian, I promised myself things would be different. Instead of jumping headfirst into a new relationship, I'd take things slowly. He was gorgeous, charming, and everything I thought I wanted in a partner, but I was determined to make him work for it. I didn't accept his first, second, or third date request. When I told him I was a single mom, he didn't even bat an eyelash. After chasing me for months, I finally agreed to go on a date with him. Everything was amazing until suddenly, it wasn't. Even with all the signs and warnings that something wasn't right, I kept charging forward. I was so in love with the idea of being in love that I was blind to everything that was wrong in the relationship.

Now, it's time for me to focus all my attention on Love. I can't uproot her life like this again. She's going to be a freshman in high school in the fall, going off to college after graduation. She has her whole life ahead of her. The only thing I seem to have ever done right in my life is be her mother.

This move will be good for both of us. A fresh start.

"Mom?"

"Yes, baby?" I croak, swiping angrily at my eyes to get rid of all evidence of my tears.

"This wasn't your fault. There was no way of knowing that Ian was hiding this big of a secret from both of us." Love strides toward me, wrapping her arms tightly around my waist.

"I know, baby." I force a smile before stepping out of her embrace and taking a seat back at the table. "Are you all packed?"

"Are you going to be alright?"

"It's rude to answer a question with a question."

"Not when my question is more important," she deadpans, crossing her arms over her chest.

"I'll be alright. I promise."

"Now, are you packed? I want to get the car loaded and headed toward Tyson's Creek before lunchtime. If we hurry, we can stop and spend the night in Memphis."

"I'm all packed. Just have to grab my backpack off the bed."

"Good," I reply, flipping the top card of the deck over on the table in front of me.

"An upright Knight of Pentacles isn't a bad card at all," Love says with a smile, her eyes glowing.

"Nope, not at all," I sigh, returning her smile as all the tension drains out of me.

I take a deep, cleansing breath as I think about what the Knight of Pentacles means—fertility and growth. The cards don't predict the future, but I have a feeling that things can only go up from here.

two

audrey

"Are we there yet?" Love asks, practically vibrating in her seat as we pull off the highway.

"We'll get there when we get there, Love."

"That's what all parents say when they have no idea." Love rolls her eyes, grabbing my phone. "It says right here that we will be there in twenty-two minutes."

"That's if I don't have to stop for gas or anything like that." I snort, loving nothing more than to push her buttons every chance I get.

"Mooom!" Love whines, dropping my phone back into the cupholder before crossing her arms over her chest and sticking out her bottom lip. "I just want to give my baby cousin a kiss hello for the first time."

"Pouting won't get us there any quicker, young lady. Besides, you remember your cousin is still inside your Aunt Bristol, right? What do you plan on kissing? Her belly?"

"Yes. And even though it won't get us there quicker,

pouting almost always gets you to stop giving me a hard time."

"Touché." I snicker, taking a moment to look at my little girl.

Ever since we left Ian's place last night, she's seemed like an entirely different child. On the outside she looks the same; her wavy black hair is piled on the top of her head in a messy bun, a few stray curls hanging out the back, brushing the shoulders of the Nirvana T-shirt she stole from my suitcase this morning. Her long legs are encased in a pair of black yoga pants—the only pants she chooses to wear—and her Converse-clad feet are propped up on the dashboard.

However, the big difference is the permanent smile plastered across her face, her hazel eyes alight with excitement at the prospect of our new adventure. It's completely the opposite of how she's been since we found out about Ian's secret family. Shame fills me as I realize I never noticed how much my relationship troubles have affected my little girl. I'm sure I shared a little too much with her about what was going on, but I needed someone to talk to about what our next step should be. She's growing up, and the decision to move has just as much to do with her as it does me.

"You realize you need to ask Bristol's permission before you go kissing her belly, right? She won't let people rub her belly, but she's going to let you give it a kiss?" I question, skeptical of my best friend's motivation.

"I already did." She smiles before pulling her phone

out of its hiding spot and shoving it in my direction. "And before you ask, you can read the text message."

BABY BEAR

We'll be there in twenty-two minutes! I need to give my baby cuz a kiss!

AUNTIE B

You want to kiss my belly?

BABY BEAR

Yes. Only once.

AUNTIE B

...

BABY BEAR

Remember that you love me and I'm your favorite niece.

AUNTIE B

You're my only niece.

BABY BEAR

I won't tell anyone...and I'll have Mom make you manicotti as soon as we get everything unpacked.

AUNTIE B

I don't want to share.

BABY BEAR

Deal. Nice doing business with you. Love you!

"Dang, you couldn't even negotiate a kiss for me too, before roping me into making her manicotti?" I shake my head at my daughter's antics.

It's no secret that she has Bristol's entire family

completely wrapped around her finger. Everyone in her family treats Love and me like we are a part of the family. If it hadn't been for my desire to stand on my own two feet, there's no doubt her parents would've adopted me, ensuring that I could travel everywhere with them.

"What can I say? She loves me more. If I had included you in our deal, she might have said no. Besides, you were gonna make her manicotti anyway. I just made sure I got something out of it."

"You aren't wrong there," I whisper, tapping Love lightly on the shoulder and pointing out the windshield, "Look at that view."

"OMG, I can't believe we get to live here," she whispers as she begins frantically taking pictures, not wanting to miss a single detail.

As we descend into Tyson's Creek, I notice the lush, rolling hills framing my new home. Off in the distance, there's a large rustic farmhouse and a few tiny cottages surrounding it. I smile as an old-fashioned wooden sign on the side of the road comes into view, and I read it aloud. "Tyson's Creek, Tennessee. Population 7,256."

Love squeals loudly before she rolls down the window and continues to take pictures of the scenery as it rolls by us. Rustic-looking buildings line the road as we inch closer to the center of town. The streets are lined with people, but no one is rushing around or in a hurry to get anywhere. Tyson's Creek looks exactly like what I envision a small, southern town being. There are a few mom-and-pop shops lining the street and no major chain stores in sight. As we drive downtown, we see The Flickhouse, the small movie theater Bristol has raved about, sitting on one corner. There's a small bookstore tucked right next to it, with Tyson's Hardware on the other side. Across the street from the theater is what looks to be a coffee shop-bakery combo named Just the Drip. A few tables are scattered in front of it, with peach-colored umbrellas open and casting shade over each table to protect the occupants from the spring sun. Right next to it is Bristol's yoga studio, Nurture Space.

"Finally, we made it." Love sighs as I pull into a parking space. We barely have time to climb out of the car before Bristol comes flying out the door, with Selina and Leia hot on her heels.

"You're here!" Bristol squeals, waddling toward us. Her bright red hair glistens in the sunlight as she throws her arms around me, bringing me in for a hug. I wrap my arms around her, careful of her adorable baby bump. Bristol is 5'5", exactly a half inch taller than me, which she always goes out of her way to point out to me, and she has curves for days. Her entire body is toned from all the yoga. The only sign she's pregnant is the small basketball-sized bump covered by her shirt, her face glowing with happiness, which makes her appear even more beautiful than usual.

"Only you could make pregnancy look good," I say, shaking my head as I pull back from her embrace. Her green eyes shine brightly with happiness; a light dusting of freckles covers the bridge of her nose, spilling onto her pink cheeks. "It seems like someone has gotten a little too much sun. You need to remember to put on sunscreen when you go out. You just look at the sun and you get burned."

"We've been telling her the same thing for months," Leia comes to a stop behind Bristol, placing her hand on her shoulder. "Not that she doesn't look amazing when she isn't pregnant."

Leia Armstrong is about two inches taller than Bristol, her blonde hair piled high on top of her head in a messy bun; a few tendrils of hair have escaped and are framing her face. She's dressed casually in a pair of black yoga pants and an oversized sweatshirt hanging slightly off her right shoulder. Her wire frame glasses are perched on the end of her nose, and thick black eyelashes frame her crystal blue eyes, which are shining with excitement.

Selina comes skidding to a stop right beside Leia; both of them are practically vibrating with excitement. This is the first time I've seen Selina Grymes in person, and she's beautiful. Her lightly tanned skin is accentuated by her chocolate brown hair, which is pulled back in a tight bun at the nape of her neck, the typical hairstyle for a ballerina. It's in drastic contrast to how she usually wears her hair, hanging loosely down her back. Selina is slightly taller than I would have expected, taller than all three of us, but I've only ever seen her in pictures sitting down, so it's not too odd. Her tiny waist is accentuated by a flowing pink dance skirt. The black leotard and pink tights she's wearing hug every curve of her body.

"Laying it on thick today, aren't we?" Bristol raises an eyebrow at Leia, causing all of us to laugh.

Leia and I have been chatting back and forth for years, ever since she and Bristol met during their junior year in college after being partnered up for a project. All the details are fuzzy, but it wasn't too long after that Bristol introduced me to Leia. Bristol declared I was her sister from another mister and demanded Leia and I be the best of friends.

When they graduated, Bristol followed Leia home to Tyson's Creek instead of chasing her parents around the country until her dad retired. It'd be a lie if I didn't say I was a little hurt that she didn't choose to come live closer to me, but it wasn't until Love was in second grade that I stopped moving around so much, finally choosing to settle down in a town near San Antonio, Texas, wanting to ensure she could make friends and thrive in school without having to worry about if she was going to see them the following year.

Once Bristol got her bearings, she combined her love for yoga and her business degree to open a yoga studio. Business has been good in this small town, thanks to everyone falling in love with her almost immediately. However, now that she's eight months pregnant, it has gotten a lot harder for her to handle a full class schedule. This created the perfect opportunity for me to escape Ian and start fresh while also helping my best friend. A win-win for everyone involved.

"Okay, I know she's your original bestie and all, but

it's my turn," Leia demands before pulling me from Bristol's grip and wrapping me tightly in a hug of her own. "I can't believe I finally get to see you in person!"

"Original bestie?" I smile, pulling back slightly and giving Selina a tiny wave.

"You knew Bristol first, hence the title *original bestie*," Leia replies matter-of-factly.

"Whatever you say."

Leia and Selina grew up here in Tyson's Creek, but Selina moved to New York to become a famous ballerina right after graduation. A few months ago, she came back to town to heal after an injury and took over the small dance studio near Nurture Space. In typical Bristol fashion, she welcomed Selina into the fold, and our little threesome became a foursome rather quickly.

Out of the three of them, I'd say I "know" Selina the least. Sure, she's joined a few of our video call gab sessions, but we've never really talked about anything too deep. It's as if she is holding us at arm's length, but I'm not sure why. Sure, she has plans on leaving town as soon as her injury heals, but that doesn't mean we can't still all be friends. Mine and Bristol's relationship survived for years with phone calls and random visits when time allowed. We are old pros at this.

"I'm so glad you finally decided to move closer to us! Hopefully, the cards didn't say anything to the contrary." Selina's hazel eyes twinkle with mirth before she winks at me, pulling me out of Leia's arms and giving me a tight squeeze.

“The outcome looks very promising, but you know the cards don’t tell the future, right?”

It took a little while for Leia and Selina to understand how people can use tarot cards to help guide their future, and, at times, I feel as if they still don’t understand, but they never use it against me. They might not believe in all that “mumbo jumbo,” as Leia loves to call it, but they both love me. Although they poke fun, it’s never meant maliciously, but that doesn’t make me any less worried about all of us being in the same place. What if I’m too weird for them? What if they hate me? Will Bristol hate me then, too?

“Now it’s time to give my baby cousin a kiss,” Love announces loudly, stopping my mind from continuing to spiral.

“Umm, Love? How do you plan to kiss your cousin?” Leia asks in confusion, her head swiveling between Bristol, Love, and me.

“I’m going to kiss her belly.”

“What!” Selina and Leia screech in unison before turning their attention toward Bristol.

“You’ve never let anyone touch your belly before, and now you’re going to let Love kiss it?” Selina mutters, putting her hands on her hips as she narrows her eyes at Bristol.

“Yeah. What she said,” Leia chimes in, causing me to giggle softly.

“She loves me more. Deal with it.” Love sticks her tongue out at the three of us before dropping to her knees and planting a kiss in the center of Bristol's belly and whispering something softly to it.

"What can I say? She promised me manicotti." Bristol shrugs her shoulders before pulling Love to her feet and pulling her in for a one-armed hug.

"You know I would've made it for you anyway, right?"

"Of course, but I can never say no to this one." Bristol plants a wet kiss on Love's forehead before whispering something into her ear.

"Really?" Love shouts before sprinting toward Selina's dance studio a few doors down.

"You stole my thunder," Selina grumbles at Bristol before turning toward me. "I have a beginner pointe class starting in about ten minutes and was planning on inviting Love to join—until someone spoiled my surprise."

"Thank you so much! Love has been a trooper about having to make this move, but she was the most upset about having to stop taking her dance classes."

"What are friends for?" Bristol smiles brightly before threading her arm through mine and leading me toward the yoga studio. "I need to make sure I remain her favorite."

"Hey, just because you're giving her a baby cousin doesn't make you her favorite!" Leia shouts after us as Selina rolls her eyes.

"Yes, it does, because someone refused to give her a baby brother. A baby cousin is the next best thing,"

Bristol comments over her shoulder as I pull us to a stop.

"Did you think about what happens if you have a girl instead of a boy?" I question, wondering the same thing.

Bristol has always wanted a little boy, claiming she has no idea what to do with a baby girl, but she has no say in the matter. The father's swimmers have everything to do with determining the sex, and if I had to hazard a guess, he probably has more girl swimmers than boy ones. I have no idea if it's true or not, but I swear I heard someone say that military spouses tend to have more girls than boys. Since the baby's father is a Marine, I'm making an educated guess. Call it wishful thinking, but when I think of Bristol being a mom, the little one is always a girl.

"Not a darn thing. Love gets a baby to snuggle, and I get free babysitting. It's a win-win for both of us."

"She has a point. Looks like we're going to need to up our game," Selina replies, pulling Leia in for a one-armed hug before she strolls toward her dance studio.

"I won't give up my favorite auntie position without a fight!" Bristol shouts.

"Neither of us expected you to," Leia says as she slides her arm through mine, and we all head toward the door of Nurture Space.

A small bell chimes as Bristol pulls the door open, and we step inside. I gasp in surprise at the breathtaking view in front of me. The entire back wall of the studio is covered in windows, natural light reaching almost every corner of the room.

"The view is perfect, isn't it?" Leia bumps her shoulder against mine.

I nod my head, unable to find the words to describe how breathtaking the view is of the same hills I saw coming into town in the background, framing the tiny town perfectly. There are several houses sprinkled in the distance, and I notice a small creek with a wooden bridge leading to another part of town.

"I knew the moment I stepped foot into this place that it was perfect." Bristol smiles as she grips my hand, pulling me further into the studio. "Let me show you around. I promise you'll love it here. Sorry it's so hot. I need to call someone to check the air conditioner."

"I really should get over to Selina's studio and check on Love." I try to pull out of her grasp, but Bristol tightens her grip.

"Love is perfectly fine. Selina wouldn't have invited her if it was any trouble. I'm sure she's probably made a few friends by now."

I pull my bottom lip between my teeth, wondering if leaving Love there is a good idea. Selina and I don't know each other very well. Yeah, we are friends, but it's not her job to watch over my daughter. She has a class to teach. The last thing she needs is an excited fourteen-year-old girl asking her a million questions while she's trying to teach. Love has a good head on her shoulders and is more mature for her age, but when she gets overly excited, she sometimes forgets her manners.

"Are you sure? I just want to pop—"

“Stop worrying.” Leia cuts me off, placing her hands on my shoulders and giving them a small squeeze. “Love is fine. It will only take a few minutes to show you around the studio, and then Bristol can go over your schedule with you.”

“But...” My eyebrows pull down as all the things that could go wrong filter through my head. My hand itches to grab the worn deck of tarot cards from my bag to see what could happen if I stayed here.

I understand this isn’t that big of a deal. The world won’t end if, by some fluke of nature, Selina has an issue with me not being there with Love. But right now, it feels like the end of the world. That no matter what decision I make, something is going to go wrong. Selina will hate me. Bristol will hate me. Leia will hate me. And the small support network I’ve scraped together will all come crumbling to the ground all because I took a few extra minutes. Love and I will be alone again.

My chest tightens, as if all the air is being sucked out of the room and someone has wrapped their fingers around my neck. I struggle to take a breath as panic bubbles up from my stomach and settles in my chest. I pull in a deep breath, willing my body to calm down, as a set of arms wrap around me.

“How about I text Selina and make sure everything is okay?” Bristol whispers before placing a kiss on the top of my head and taking a step back.

“That will work perfectly.” I sigh, all the tension

leaving my body as Bristol pulls her phone out and sends off a quick message.

It only takes a few moments before Selina answers and Bristol reads it to me. "Love has hit it off with another girl around her age in the class." She looks up from her phone, "We might as well get started with the tour because the class Selina wanted Love to sit in on is about to start."

"That's plenty of time to tour the rest of the studio and then treat me to a coffee at Just the Drip on the corner," Leia says, threading her arm through mine.

"Shouldn't you be treating me since it's my first day in town?"

"Semantics." Leia waves her hand, dismissing my comments

It doesn't take too much time for Bristol and Leia to show me around. There are two rooms off to the right of the main studio for the smaller classes Bristol offers during the week. Off to the other side, there is a small break room with a refrigerator, a two-person table, and a microwave tucked into the corner.

"This place is bigger than I thought," I say as we step back into the reception area.

"I've done a lot of expanding over the years. Thankfully, Selina has a certain construction company owner wrapped around her pinkie finger." Leia winks at Bristol before taking a seat in one of the chairs scattered around the area.

"There must be a story there."

"There is, but it's Selina's story to tell," Bristol replies, pulling off a sticky note and scribbling something on it before handing it to me. "Here is your schedule for the rest of this week. It's only one class, but I have a doctor's appointment and would really hate to cancel it. We can sit down after that and divide up the classes so it's the best fit for both of our schedules."

"That sounds perfect. But don't think I forgot about that juicy bit of information you just dropped into my lap."

"Don't worry, Audrey. I'll give you the *Reader's Digest* version over coffee," Leia chimes in, causing Bristol to scowl in her direction.

"Deal," I reply. "I just want to check in on Love to see if she needs anything. She left her cell and everything in the car when she took off."

"You're such a good mom." Bristol sniffs before wrapping her arms around me in a tight hug.

"I try."

"No, you are." She pulls back, unshed tears shining back at me. "I hope that I'm half as good of a mother to this little one as you are to Love."

"Aww, you're going to make me cry."

"Please, no crying," Leia says as we break apart. "If you cry, then she's going to cry, and then I'll start crying, and then I'll never get my coffee."

"Heaven forbid you're deprived of your coffee." We both wave at Bristol before heading out the door and toward the dance studio and walk right in.

"Can I help you?" I turn, noticing a young woman in her early twenties, about my height with beautiful golden-brown skin, sitting behind the small receptionist desks. Her dark hair is pulled into a tight bun on top of her head. She looks just like the photos of Misty Copeland that Love had hung all over her room.

"Selina brought my daughter, Love, to view one of her classes. Do you know if she's still here?"

"Of course." She gives me a warm, reassuring smile. "You must be Audrey."

"Yes, the one and only," Leia answers, as if my arrival in town was big news.

"I've heard nothing but good things from Ms. Selina, Bristol, and Leia about you. They've all been talking nonstop about your arrival for weeks now. I'm so glad to finally meet you."

"They've been talking about me?"

"Of course we have! We've been trying to get you to move your butt here since Bristol and I came back from college." Leia throws her arm over my shoulder and pulls me into her side. "Once Selina came back to town, we wanted all of us together in one place, just like the four musketeers."

"You know there were only three musketeers, right?" The girl behind the counter snickers quietly before holding her hand out toward me. "I'm Emersyn."

"Nice to meet you." She gives me a slight nod before all three of us laugh.

Emersyn glances at the clock. "If you're here for Love,

the class won't end for another thirty minutes. There's a coffee shop nearby. You could grab a snack and maybe some coffee since you've had such a long drive."

"And that's where we're headed, but someone wanted to check in on Love before we went."

"If it's not too much trouble, can you please ask Love to come find me at the coffee shop next door if I'm not back by the time class is over?"

"No trouble at all." Emersyn smiles brightly. "We all look out for each other here in Tyson's Creek."

"That we do, but we also have a tendency to be in each other's business." Leia rolls her eyes, causing me to snicker softly. "Everyone means well, but there's not much else here to do besides gossip."

"Speaking of gossip, you have a story to tell me in exchange for your coffee fix. I can come back and sign Love up for dance classes later," I reply as I grab a small piece of paper and begin writing my phone number.

"That I do. Catch you later, Em."

"See you, Leia."

"If there is any trouble at all, here is my phone number. Just call me, and I'll come running."

"I promise, although I don't think there will be any problems." Emersyn winks at me playfully as I turn and head for the door.

"Thanks." I give her a slight wave before heading out the door with Leia.

three

connor

"The delay won't be too bad, but we were already cutting it close." My best friend and business partner, Vance, groans as he flops down into his seat. "We may have to call the client about there being a delay."

I stare at him, wondering when his chair is going to break. His large body leans back in the chair as he props his work boots on the edge of the desk. Little pieces of dirt flake onto the surface and floor, making an even bigger mess of his work area.

"You really shouldn't put your feet on the desk, especially when they are covered in mud."

"They aren't covered in mud," he mutters as he runs his hand through his dark hair, making it stand up in every direction before pulling his feet down and placing them on the floor. "Now, explain how we are going to fix this problem."

His brown eyes narrow in my direction as I run my hand down my face before focusing on the spreadsheet in front of me. I wince, knowing he won't like the solution

I've come up with. "We can use some of the lumber we originally ordered to finish up the addition to your house's remodel so the renovations on the client's house are completed on time."

"Sure, what's another few weeks' delay in finishing the dream home for Selina?"

"Don't be like that, Vance. You've been slowly renovating that house in hopes of Selina coming home. Another few weeks before we can finish the addition won't change a thing."

Vance has been working on fixing up Selina's and his dream home for the last few years. He promised her they would grow old together in this house, sitting on what I can only describe as a porch bed, which used to be at her parents' house until they gave it to him. Too bad for him that the day before our high school graduation, Selina left for New York to become a prima ballerina without a word, leaving Vance alone here with nothing but their dreams.

"True, but it's not like I can finish the renovations without her input. I just need something to keep my mind off the fact that she doesn't plan on giving me the time of day any time soon." He winks at me before checking his watch. "Hey, don't you have somewhere you have to be?"

I glance at my watch and curse. "You're right. I need to pick up Jade from dance class. Sorry I'm leaving a mess for you to clean up. I owe you one."

"Don't sweat it, man. Go take care of my niece. But

you're right, you owe me." Vance claps me on the shoulder as I grab my keys and head toward my truck.

As I rush to pick up my daughter, I think back to a time when things were perfect. Lydia was my greatest love before Jade was born. Vance, Selina, Lydia, and I were thick as thieves, the best of friends, until one day, we were something more. It was as if I woke up one morning and knew that Lydia was the woman I wanted to spend the rest of my life with. People always said we were meant to be together, but we had been friends for so long that I didn't want to risk our friendship by confessing my feelings. Luckily for me, Lydia was brave enough for both of us and figured out my true feelings quickly.

I remember the day she came storming up to me before class, demanding to know if I loved her. I hesitated for only a moment before wrapping my arms tightly around her and crushing my lips against hers, pouring all my feelings into that single kiss, hoping I could tell her everything I'd been too afraid to say for years. We broke apart, breathing heavily, and she said, "Took you long enough," before bringing our lips together a second time, and the rest was history.

We graduated from high school and got married. Neither one of us wanted anything fancy in life. Vance and I started a construction business together while I took online business classes at night. Those early years were hard, but we made it through. Now Ace & Hammer Builders is one of the leading companies in the area. We do everything from regular handyman work to general contracting for everyone in Tyson's Creek and the neighboring areas.

About a year after we were married, Lydia discovered she was pregnant. I was over the moon, secretly wishing for a little girl that looked exactly like her mother. Lydia and I were nervous about being first-time parents, but thankfully, we had our family and friends to help us. It really does take a village to raise a child, and our village was solid. As Lydia's delivery date grew closer, we got the normal first-time parent jitters. We asked the doctor a million questions about possible complications with delivery, but they assured us everything was going perfectly. Our baby was in perfect health, and we were anxiously waiting for them to arrive. But things aren't always as they seem.

One night, the week before Lydia's due date, she wasn't feeling the best. She had been experiencing contractions most of the day, but nothing that led us to believe she was in labor. However, as we got closer to bedtime, they were becoming stronger and more frequently. We immediately called the doctor, but he stated that since the pain was still bearable and her water had not broken, we had a few hours before we needed to head to the hospital. He suggested we get some rest, but if anything changed, then we should immediately head to the hospital.

We ended up staying awake for a few more hours, anxiously waiting for our baby to arrive, but ultimately headed to bed to get some sleep. A few hours later, I was woken up by Lydia gasping for air and clutching her chest. She was pale, beads of sweat pebbling on her forehead as she fought to breathe. I felt helpless, unable to do anything but hold her hand and watch her continue to suffer.

At first, I thought she was having a panic attack, which wasn't odd for her in the last few months, so I focused on helping her get her breathing under control, but the moment she began vomiting uncontrollably, we knew something serious had happened. I scooped her into my arms and rushed her to the hospital, but by then, it was already too late.

The emergency room doctor said that Lydia was having an Amniotic Fluid Embolism (AFE) and was dying. Apparently, she was, in fact, in labor, but because of a severe allergic reaction to the amniotic fluid, she was dying. They needed to work quickly to deliver our baby, or I could lose them both.

I felt as if the world was collapsing around me, unable to wrap my head around what was happening. We had just spoken to the doctor a few hours before. He assured us that everything was fine and that he'd see us at our appointment later in the week. *Fine?* Everything was *not* fine. The birth of our child was supposed to be the second happiest moment of my life, but instead, I was holding my wife's hair back as she dry heaved into a toilet, fighting for her and our baby's life.

As they wheeled her out of the room for a c-section, she had a bright smile on her face as she reassured me that everything was going to work out, but deep down, I knew it would never be the same. While I wanted to go into the operating room, the surgeon wouldn't allow it, so I stayed in the waiting room. I paced back and forth around the room, my mind filled with every possible outcome, but I never could've prepared myself for the moment the doctor laid my baby girl in my arms and told me the love of my life had died giving birth to our daughter, Jade.

That was fourteen years ago, give or take a few months. Since then, it's been Jade and me against the world. People feared I would shun Jade, resenting her for her mother's death, but I never did. It made me want to hold on to the last piece of Lydia I had, our little girl. It was hard raising a little girl on my own, but thankfully, I had friends and family there to support me, helping me through the hard times and celebrating the good right along with me.

The shrill ring of my cell phone breaks me from the painful memories. "Connor Bennett."

"Always so formal when you answer the phone." I smile as Bristol's voice filters over the line.

"What can I do for you, Bristol? Are you having trouble with the new thermostat we installed a few days ago?"

"Unfortunately, yes. It's hotter than Satan's house cat in here. I followed all the instructions on how to turn it on, but it's not cooling down."

I chuckle softly before replying. "Alright, I have to pick up Jade from dance class. I can stop by and take a quick look. If it's anything serious, I can come back in a few days to do the repairs."

"Hopefully, it's nothing too serious. I don't want to cancel classes for the rest of the week."

"I'm sure it's nothing more than operator error. You aren't the best at dealing with electronic equipment."

"Ain't that the truth, but I really didn't do anything this time." Bristol pauses for a moment before continuing. "Audrey and her daughter arrived today..." Her voice trails off slightly as I shake my head.

"I'm glad you finally have someone to help you at the studio."

After all these years, I can see a setup coming a mile away. This isn't the first time someone has tried to set me up with one of their friends. According to them, I'm a catch. A successful business owner, I own my own home, and apparently, I'm not hard on the eyes either. But ever since the day Jade was born, she's been the only girl in my life. I don't have time for anything else, let alone taking some woman I'll never speak to again to dinner. I'd rather be at home, watching a movie with Jade, than anywhere else in this world. She's the last piece of Lydia I have left, and I'm going to do everything in my power to ensure she has everything she needs.

Bristol sighs. "There's nothing wrong with finding someone to spend some time with, Connor."

"If I had time, I'd find someone. Jade is my number one priority." My words are clipped, but I know she means well. Everyone does. My friends and family only want me to be happy, but no one interests me. I gave my heart to Lydia when we barely knew what love was. I won't settle for anything less than that feeling again. It's rare for a person to find a love like ours once during their lifetime. It's completely insane to think that it could happen to me a second time.

"I'll leave it, but you can't forget to live your life. Lydia wouldn't have wanted that," she replies softly.

"I am living my life, Bristol." I sigh, pulling into a spot near the dance studio. "I'll see you in a little while to check the thermostat."

I have a few minutes before Jade finishes dance class, so I decide to stop at the coffee shop for her favorite dessert. I'm pretty sure I'm going to have to work this weekend because of the delays. When you're one of the only construction companies in town, you're never hurting for business. However, that also means we're always busy. Even though I've managed to find a solution for our late lumber shipment, we still have guys who have lives outside of this business. Sure, we could call them in, asking them to sacrifice time with their families, but we try not to if we can help it. Sometimes, it falls on Vance and me to pick up the slack.

Jade and I had made plans to go camping this weekend with her uncle Vance, but that's out of the question now that we have to rearrange our entire schedule for the coming week. Jade is going to be beyond disappointed that she'll be spending the weekend stuck with me at the construction site. But I'm not above bribing her to gain forgiveness.

The bell above the door of Just the Drip rings, and I step right into a line, waiting patiently to order. This place has been around since I was in high school. Although it's changed hands a couple of times, it hasn't changed much. The cozy atmosphere gives students and business people a place to meet while also making it feel like home at the same time.

As I look around the space, my eyes lock on a woman I've never seen before sitting at a small table near the front window. My breath catches as I stare at her sipping her coffee. Her curly hair is pushed back from her face by a headband. The sunlight filters through the large window to her left, casting an angelic glow across her profile as she brings her coffee up to her perfect lips.

I force myself to face forward, remaining focused on the person behind the counter taking orders, but my eyes keep drifting back to the mysterious beauty at the table. My heart pounds inside my chest as I fight the urge to step out of line and head directly toward her table, wanting to know everything about her.

I give my head a shake, attempting to clear my mind of this mysterious woman. She's just another pretty face, nothing more, nothing less. I'm male, so of course I'm going to notice how breathtakingly beautiful she is, but nothing can come of this attraction I feel toward her. Jade is my number one priority, and dating isn't in the cards for me.

"Get your shit together, Connor. She isn't the first pretty woman you've ever seen," I mumble to myself as I step up to the counter to place my order.

"Can I get you your usual, Mr. Bennett?" Katie says with a bright smile.

"That would be great," I reply, my eyes shifting to the right, hoping to catch sight of the woman before I snap them back to Katie. "But how many times do I have to tell you to call me Connor?"

"A million, but if my mom ever found out I called you by your first name, she'd tan my backside." She snickers before keying in my order.

"Fair enough."

"Can I get you anything else?"

"Can I also get an apple cinnamon scone and one of those fancy lattes Jade always orders?"

"Sucking up to Jade?"

"Is it that obvious?" I chuckle, reaching into my back pocket for my wallet.

"Only to someone who knows you and your daughter very well."

"That would be you and everyone else in town."

Living in a small town has its perks. Everyone is there for each other when you need them. Katie and her parents moved in next door to us when Jade was five or six years old, and she was the perfect age for babysitting. Although I never went out on dates, I had the occasional business dinner or late night at the office. Katie was a great option when last-minute things came up. Living next door made it easier for her and Jade to spend time together, and I never had to worry about there not being someone right there if something happened. It was a win-win for both of us.

"By the way, her name is Audrey. She just moved here from Texas with her daughter to help Bristol at the yoga studio," Katie says, her eyes shifting toward the woman before a sly smile spreads across her face.

"Who?"

"The woman sitting in the corner that you haven't stopped staring at since you walked in here."

"Was I that obvious?" I chuckle, gripping the back of my neck in embarrassment.

"Only to someone who's paying attention," Katie replies, placing the two drinks into a carrier and sliding it across the counter before handing me a bag with Jade's treat inside. "You should go talk to her."

"I don't date."

"Who said anything about a date? Everyone needs friends."

"Friends? Maybe," I respond quickly and grab my purchases, turning on my heels to head toward the door.

I focus on the door, needing to get out of here as quickly as possible and far away from this mystery woman and all the emotions her appearance has stirred up inside me. Instead, I take a hard left and head toward her. It's as if I'm moving on autopilot, having no idea how I made it to the opposite side of the café without making a complete fool of myself.

I stop just short of colliding with her table, standing there, waiting for her to look up at me, but her eyes are focused on her phone. My stomach knots as my palms sweat, wondering what the hell I'm doing here. I haven't had a conversation with a member of the opposite sex, who wasn't a friend or family member, since Lydia passed. Am I supposed to get her phone number or ask Bristol for information about her before even trying to talk to her? I have no idea what I'm doing, but instead of turning around and heading out the door, I clear my throat, hoping to get her attention.

"Hello." She smiles brightly, a dimple appearing on her right cheek.

My brain seems to cease all function the moment our eyes meet. She's even more beautiful up close. She looks to be around my age, evident by the way her brown skin crinkles around her eyes, her curly hair lands just below her shoulder blades, with hints of gold and red shimmering in the sunlight that is coming through the window beside her, and a nice pair of slightly pink, pouty lips call to me. I stand transfixed by her beauty, unable to find a way to stop her from leaving. Every part of my being wants to be near her, yearning to hear the sound of her voice.

I open and close my mouth a few times, trying to find my voice, before I finally manage to greet her properly.

"Hi," I choke out. The gravelly sound of my voice has me clearing my throat. "I noticed you sitting here all alone and was wondering if you'd like some company?"

What the hell? This woman knows nothing about me, and here I am, throwing myself at her like a hormonal teenage boy. I swallow hard, unable to tear my eyes away from her as her smile slowly begins to fade.

"Umm, that's nice of you, but I really should get going." Her eyebrows pull down in concern as she grabs her bag from the chair beside her and pushes back from the table.

She has every right to be wary of me. Hell, if Jade was in this situation, I'd tell her to run, not walk, in the other direction and never look back. I should give her some space, but it's as if we are two magnets being drawn closer to each other. There's just something about her that makes me want to say something to reassure her that I mean no harm.

"I'm not a creep. I noticed you sitting here the moment I walked into the café, and I haven't been able to stop looking at you. I know it sounds weird, but I couldn't bring myself to leave here without saying hello."

My hand tightens around the drink carrier, worried that she's going to walk away without saying another word, but she does the exact opposite.

"How sweet." Her cheeks pink slightly as she flashes me a shy smile. "My name is Audrey Wilde. It's a pleasure to meet you," she whispers softly, her caramel-colored eyes locking with mine.

"Hello, Audrey." I place the bag and coffee on the table before reaching out my hand toward her. "I'm Connor Bennett. And the pleasure is all mine."

She places her hand gently in mine. As soon as our skin connects, an electric current sizzles up my arm. Her eyes widen in surprise as she pulls her lip between her teeth before dropping her head downward. The spot over my heart aches at the thought of not being able to catch another glimpse of her beautiful eyes. My hand moves on its own, resting my finger below her chin and forcing her to look at me a second time.

"Daddy!"

I reluctantly pull my eyes away from Audrey and take a step back. My entire body tenses as I watch Jade come running toward me. She is the spitting image of her mother, with the same long dark hair and lithe form. The only thing she inherited from me is the color of my green eyes; the rest is all her mother.

I wonder what she would think seeing me this close to another woman. Will she be angry or upset at the idea of bringing someone else into our lives? Worried that I was forgetting her mother? I brace myself for her harsh words, but then I catch sight of the bright smile as it spreads across her face, setting me at ease almost immediately.

"Hey, baby girl. How did you know I was here?" I smile at Jade before wrapping my arms around her and planting a kiss on the top of her head.

"I had no idea you'd be here, but I'd be lying if I said I was surprised." She rises on her toes and plants a kiss on my cheek. "I had to show my new friend, Love, where this place was. Selina told us her mom said to meet her here."

"That was nice of you." I hold my hand out for her to shake. "It's nice to meet you, Love. I'm Connor, Jade's Dad."

She gives me a skeptical look before tentatively shaking my hand.

"How was class today?"

"It was amazing! I'm so excited about tryouts in a few weeks. I'm a shoo-in for the lead role." Jade pulls from my embrace and turns to address Love standing next to her. "No offense, Love. If you got the part, I'd be happy for you. But I really want the lead role this year."

The girl replies with a bright smile. "None taken. Although I doubt I'd get it anyway."

"Don't talk like that, sweetie. You're an amazing dancer. They'd be lucky to have you as the lead," Audrey chimes in as she wraps the young girl in her arms, pulling her tightly against her chest.

"What were you two doing before we arrived?" Love questions, her eyes narrowing slightly as they flick between her mother and me.

"Talking," I respond quickly, not knowing how to describe what had just happened between Audrey and me.

"That looked like a lot more than just talking..." Jade raises her eyebrow at me, crossing her arms over her chest.

"Yes, just talking," Audrey squeaks, picking up her mug and finishing the contents in one swallow. "It was nice meeting you, Connor, but we have to get going."

"Bye, Jade." Love waves at both of us over her shoulder before following Audrey out the door.

I realize I have no way to get a hold of her. Should I have asked for her phone number? Her email address? Is that even what people do these days? I don't have the slightest clue how to go about getting to know a woman or even why I'm so interested in this complete stranger. No one has ever piqued my interest the way Audrey has after only speaking to her for a few minutes. Could it be something as simple as her being a new face in town, or could it be something more?

People have been telling me for years that I shouldn't close myself off to love just because Lydia passed away, but is it really okay for me to be feeling like this? Is the desire I already feel toward Audrey only natural? A part of me sees my entire interaction with Audrey as wrong, that I'm betraying the memory of Lydia and the love we shared because of a pretty face and a gorgeous smile. Lydia meant the world to me. She was the person I promised to spend the rest of my life loving, the mother of my child, but there's another part of me that wants to explore the connection between Audrey and me.

"Earth to Dad?" Jade's voice brings me back to the present. "What's going on?"

"Nothing. Bristol called and told me her friend had arrived. When I saw someone in the coffee shop I didn't recognize, I assumed it was her and introduced myself. I was just being friendly."

"Yeah, sure." Jade pats my arm before pointing toward the bag sitting on the table. "Is that for me?"

"Yes," I respond quickly, grabbing the bag and handing it to her.

"Good. First, tell me whatever it is that's going to upset me, and then you can tell me everything that happened between you and Love's mom." Jade walks around the table and drops into Audrey's vacant seat.

"I was just introducing myself."

"Tell that to someone who doesn't know you, Dad. The way you were looking at Audrey seemed like a lot more than just being friendly."

"And what if it was?"

"More than just being friendly?" she questions, taking a sip of her drink.

I nod my head, wanting to know what Jade thinks about me finding another woman attractive. It's always been us against the world. What she thinks about whatever just happened between Audrey and me is important. One word from her and this thing could end before it even has a chance to get started.

"Then you definitely need to tell me everything that happened because you're going to need all the help you can get."

"Either way, Squirt, I need to stop at the yoga studio and look at Bristol's thermostat. She said it wasn't working. Can we table this conversation for later?"

"Yes, but don't think I'm going to forget." She huffs,

grabbing her coffee and treat off the stable and heading toward the door.

I sigh loudly, sending up a silent prayer of thanks for this momentary reprieve from my daughter's interrogation. There is no way I'll be able to talk my way out of having this conversation with Jade. Hopefully, Jade doesn't say a word about my interaction with Audrey when we are with Bristol, or I'll never hear the end of it from either of them. Besides, there really isn't much for me to tell them besides Audrey Wilde is one of the most gorgeous women I have ever seen.

"Bristol..." I say to myself, suddenly remembering I have the perfect way to get all the information about Audrey Wilde that I need.

four

connor

The moment I open the door to Nurture Space, Jade makes a beeline for Bristol. "My dad has the hots for your friend, Audrey, and needs all the information he can get about her."

"Oh, he does. Does he?" Bristol wraps her arms around Jade, giving her a quick hug.

"Yup. Those two almost set Just the Drip on fire with the way they were looking at each other. Love and I came in at the perfect time to stop them from going at it right there on one of the tables."

"Don't listen to her," I grunt, my face heating slightly and my stomach knotting as Bristol's gaze settles on me. "You need to stop exaggerating things, Jade. You're going to give Bristol the wrong idea about me and her friend."

"The only wrong idea that I could give her is that you aren't interested, and we both know that's a load of crap," Jade snaps back before plopping into an empty chair. "Just admit you like her, Dad. Then ask Bristol to tell you everything you need to know to make her fall in love with you."

"I don't need her to fall in love with me," I grumble, wanting nothing more than for the ground to open and swallow me whole. I'm a grown man. The last thing I need is for my teenage daughter to be meddling in my social life.

"So, you do like her?"

"I never said that. Stop putting words into my mouth, Jade."

Shame and anger surges through me at the budding feelings I have for Audrey Wilde. I promised to love, honor, and cherish Lydia until the day I died, yet here I am, thinking about starting a relationship with the first woman I find even remotely attractive in years.

"Cut your dad some slack, Jade. If he wants our help with figuring out whatever is going on between him and Audrey, then he'll ask. Right, Connor?"

"Right," I respond gruffly, heading further into the studio. "I'm going to go check the thermostat. Jade, stay out of trouble."

I stop in front of the thermostat and mindlessly press buttons, attempting to get this thing to turn on and work properly. However, instead of paying attention to what I'm doing, my mind wanders back to my conversation with Jade.

I don't know how to describe these foreign feelings that have overtaken my mind since I laid eyes on Audrey. She intrigues me, and I want to know everything I can about her. I want to know why she moved to Tyson's Creek and what her favorite movies are. Anything that can explain this pull I feel toward her, something I haven't felt since I admitted to myself that I was in love with Lydia.

Shame fills me as I think of my dead wife. Lydia meant everything to me. She was the love of my life. The mother of my child. Allowing myself to have romantic feelings for anyone else feels like a betrayal of some sort. Like I'm turning my back on the love we had for each other by even thinking about another woman romantically. However, Lydia's biggest joy in life was ensuring the people around her were happy. She'd do anything in her power to ensure that happened, and I was no different. Everything she did was to ensure her own happiness as well as our happiness together, and I did the same. But even thinking about Audrey makes my heart ache for what I lost at the same time.

"Penny for your thoughts?"

I turn and find Bristol leaning against the open doorway to one of the smaller studios, her eyes narrowing slightly as she studies me.

"There has to be something wrong with the unit. I should be able to come back in a few days and take a look."

I don't want to have this conversation with anyone, let alone the object of all my inner turmoil's best friend. Bristol and I are close, but she and Audrey have been friends since they were kids, that much I know. I'm sure her loyalty lies with Audrey and Love, but she might be the only person in all of Tyson's Creek who can give me the answers I'm searching for when it comes to Audrey Wilde.

"Thanks, but that's not what I was asking."

"Okay..." My voice trails off as I push one more button on the keypad and turn toward her.

"Audrey."

Just the mention of her name sends my heart racing in my chest, my stomach tying itself in knots. How can someone I just met have this much control over me without even being in the same room? I silently chastise myself for my absurd reaction, willing my heart to calm down. I haven't spoken more than a few words to this woman. Sure, she's gorgeous, but there's no need to be acting like this.

"What about her?" My voice raises slightly as I try to walk past Bristol, but she grabs my arm.

"Don't play dumb with me, Connor Bennett! I may not have known you all my life like everyone else, but I can tell when there's something bothering you." I turn toward her. Bristol's eyes narrow slightly as she looks me up and down, waiting patiently for me to answer her.

I had planned on fixing the thermostat and heading home to eat dinner and watch a movie with Jade, but Bristol won't let this go, especially after Jade's bout of word vomit when we first arrived. They both know something happened between Audrey and me, so there's no sense hiding it. But maybe she might be able to help me make sense of these emotions swirling through my mind.

"Everything is bothering me." I sigh, all the fight draining from my body. "That's the problem."

"Okay, start at the beginning."

I peer around the corner, checking to make sure Jade is okay, and find her sitting in a chair tucked into the corner. Her eyes are focused on her phone. I open my mouth to call out to her and notice a small earbud tucked into her ear, and I chuckle. Jade is occupied for the time being, and since she has her earbuds in, there's no chance of her overhearing my conversation with Bristol. It's embarrassing enough to be talking to her about this. I'd rather not also have to explain all this to my teenage daughter at the same time. I take a deep breath before I unload everything onto Bristol, hoping she can help me make some sense of everything that has happened in the last few hours.

"The moment I laid eyes on Audrey sitting in the café, I felt like I couldn't breathe. She literally took my breath away. I tried to remain focused on what I went there for, but I couldn't stop looking at her. It got so bad that Katie called me out on staring and told me who she was. I tried to leave like a normal human, but I couldn't resist the urge to speak to her and almost made a complete ass out of myself. Then it was as if I forgot how to speak, let alone why I suddenly wanted to know everything about her. In great detail. Instead, I just stood there like a statue, unable to speak or even think of anything but her. Honestly, if Jade and Love hadn't walked in when they did, I probably would have kissed her right there in front of the whole town."

"Oh." Bristol's eyes widen in surprise as a mischievous smile spreads across her face.

"Yeah, *oh*. I should run as far as I can away from this woman, but every time I think about never speaking to her again, my heart aches."

"You like her."

"But I just met her," I reply quickly, not understanding where these feelings are coming from.

I had known Lydia almost all our lives, but it wasn't until we were in high school that I had any type of romantic feelings for her. I'm sure we could blame the timing on puberty, but loving her was like breathing. Since we had known each other for so long, I knew everything I needed to know about her to decide that I loved her. But I've only talked to Audrey for a few seconds. Other than my very physical reaction to seeing her for the first time, there's nothing else to base my feelings on. Yes, she is beautiful. There's no denying that, but can I really discover that I have feelings for someone just by looking at them?

"I haven't even spoken more than a few words to her. How can I possibly have feelings for someone I just met?"

"I'm not saying that you should get down on one knee and profess your undying love for her tomorrow. But you are attracted to her. There's something about Audrey Wilde that sets your heart ablaze, a yearning that has settled deep in your soul."

"Yeah, that's one way to put it."

"So, what's the problem, then?"

"Jade." I reach back and rub the back of my neck, peeking around the corner again to check on my daughter.

"Connor." Bristol sighs. "I know this might come as a shock to you, but Jade is going to be a freshman in high school in the fall. I doubt she will have anything against you dating someone."

"But I don't want her to feel neglected or forgotten." I groan, pacing back and forth in the hallway, trying to calm all this nervous energy swirling inside me. "I haven't dated anyone since Lydia passed away. First, I was focused on finishing my business degree and getting the construction company up and running. Then, every person someone tried to introduce me to wasn't right. Jade is the only thing I have left of Lydia; I don't want to tarnish her memory by bringing another woman into our lives."

"Ah, now everything makes more sense." She steps in front of me, causing me to stop abruptly, and places both of her hands on my shoulders. "Lucky for you, there's a very easy solution for all your problems."

"And what is that?"

"Ask her."

"Ask who?"

"Jade." I open my mouth to respond, but she places her hand over my mouth. "Before you say anything, hear me out."

I nod my head, waiting patiently for her to continue.

She stares at me for a few minutes before she pulls her hand away. When I don't say a word, she speaks again.

"You've raised Jade to be an amazing young woman. Sure, she's still a teenager, but Jade has no problem articulating her wants and feelings to you. All you need to do is ask her."

Bristol is right. Jade isn't one to mince words or not speak her mind. If she had a problem with whatever happened between Audrey and me at the café, she'd have said something by now. Instead, she was all about trying to help me not make a complete fool out of myself, even going as far as enlisting Bristol's help in figuring all of this out. I still need to have a serious conversation with her about it, but the reminder to trust my daughter to let me know her thoughts and feelings was a much-needed one. Sometimes, I forget that my little girl has grown into a strong-willed and beautiful woman.

"I also think you're getting too far ahead of yourself. You just met Audrey and know nothing about her. She's had a rough go since Love was born. She has some major scars that need to heal before she'll be ready to open herself up to falling in love, but that doesn't mean you can't be friends."

"Jade and Love seemed to have hit it off," I mumble, my mind wandering back to how the two girls interacted with each other in Just the Drip.

If I didn't know better, I'd have thought they'd known each other for years. Jade makes friends easily, wanting to ensure everyone feels welcome, similar to her mother, but she's gone beyond that with Love. She considered how something she said might have affected her, while also taking the time to encourage her to try out for the lead, even though Jade has been practicing nonstop to ensure she has the lead in the bag this year.

"Exactly, get to know Audrey. Maybe you'll discover you don't want the relationship to move any further."

"What if I discover I want more?"

"Then you will figure out a way to make it happen, but don't stress about it right now. Just let things happen naturally."

"Okay, I think I can do that."

Bristol smiles brightly at me before threading her arm through mine and handing me a piece of paper. "And friends have each other's numbers and addresses."

"Are you sure she's okay with this?"

"The moment you left the room to go fix the thermostat, Jade begged me for Love's number. As I was writing it down, I let it slip that Audrey and Love were moving into your neighborhood, and naturally, she wanted their address next."

"Why didn't you give this to her?"

"Because I also need a favor." Bristol shoots me a pleading look as we come to a stop in the lobby right in front of the door. "Audrey has a hard time asking for help, so I know she'll be trying to unpack her entire house by herself. Since you live in the same neighborhood, I hoped you would swing by and give her a hand when her delivery arrives tomorrow."

"That won't be a problem at all," I reply, my mind already coming up with ways that I could drop by Audrey's place and not seem like a total stalker.

"Did you fix the thermostat?" Jade questions as she pulls her earbuds from her ears and pushes to her feet.

"Kind of. I think there is something wrong with the unit itself." I wrap my arm around her shoulders, pulling her in for a one-armed hug and planting a kiss on the top of her head.

"That sounds very expensive." Bristol pulls her lip between her teeth, worry written all over her face.

"Don't stress. It should be an easy fix, and I think we have all the parts we need at the office, but you should really think about getting a new unit before more costly repairs arise."

"With the baby coming soon, I've been trying to save as much as I can, but since I won't have to close the shop after the baby is born because Audrey's here, I should be able to swing a new unit in the winter."

"I'm sure the baby's father wouldn't mind helping." Jade smacks me hard on the shoulder, scowling at me before putting a finger over her mouth.

Bristol has been tight-lipped about who the father of her baby is. The only thing she'll tell any of us is that he isn't from here or in the picture. I'm not sure if the poor guy even knows she's pregnant with his child, but it's not my place to say anything. The only thing any of us can do is keep supporting Bristol and be there for her if she needs anything.

"Shut up, Dad. You know baby daddy is a sore subject. One harsh word from Bristol could send Audrey running."

"Your dad is only looking out for us, Jade." She runs her hand across her belly before pointing her finger at me. "But he won't continue to push his luck because he remembers the baby and I have everything we need right here. You two, Selina, Vance, Leia, Audrey, and Love. You guys are our family."

"That's right!" Jade runs toward her, wrapping her arms around her shoulder and planting a wet kiss on her cheek. "I'm like a fungus. You're never getting rid of me."

"An incredibly adorable fungus." Bristol gives Jade a tight squeeze before pushing her in my direction. "Now, you two get out of here so I can close up shop and head home for the night."

"I'll come by later in the week to do the repairs on the unit."

"Depending on the day, Audrey might be working. Just let me know what day you plan on coming in so I can let her know." Bristol holds the door open, letting Jade and me exit. "Thanks so much for doing this for me. I know you guys are in your busy season right now."

"Call us even. Thanks for the pep talk."

"No need to thank me. Just promise me you'll be careful with both of your hearts."

five

audrey

"You and Jade seemed to have become fast friends." I break the silence that has settled between Love and me since we walked out of the small café a few minutes ago. "Maybe you two will have some of the same classes."

Seeing Jade and Love coming into the coffee shop together was amazing. Love has always been on the shy side around people she doesn't know. To say I worried about her making friends after the move would be an understatement, but seeing those two together warmed my heart. It reminded me of the first time I met Bristol. Her bright red hair shone in the sunlight as she came barreling toward me at the bus stop. I was standing alone, away from everyone else, under a tree. As usual, my nose was stuck in a book, but she didn't care. She started talking to me like we were the best of friends, rambling on about some show on television, and she hasn't left my side since.

"She's awesome, Mom." Love smiles brightly as she comes to a stop in front of Barre Studio. "The moment I walked into class with Auntie Selina, she came right up to me, introduced herself, and said we were going to be best friends."

"Best friends, huh?" I snicker softly at the expression on Love's face.

"Ha, that's what I said. She said she heard everything she needed to know about me from Auntie Selina and Auntie Bristol."

Although Love and I are similar in most ways, when it comes to our emotions, we couldn't be more opposite. Where I wear my heart on my sleeve, she keeps hers close to her chest. I trust anyone at their word, but Love is skeptical until proven otherwise. However, once you get through all the safeguards she has around her heart, she's the most loyal person you've ever met. I just hope Jade proves to be someone worthy of that devotion. I have a good feeling about her, but I'm not sure I'm the best judge of someone's character.

"Sounds more like a relationship than being best friends." My eyes widen as her smile dulls slightly, realizing how she must have taken my statement. "Not that there's anything wrong with that. No matter who you choose to have a relationship with, I'll support you."

"I know, Mom." Love shakes her head as she rolls her eyes at me. "But Jade and I will never be anything besides friends unless you and her dad hit it off."

"Subtle segue, Love," I mumble before pulling the door open and motioning for Love to head inside.

"I thought so myself." She flashes me a smug smile before stepping through the door.

I flex my hand at my side as I'm reminded of my strange encounter with Connor in the Just the Drip. I smile at the memory of how awkward and out of sorts he seemed when he stopped next to my table. At first, I thought it was someone asking if they could take the vacant chair, but when he asked to join me, I froze. When I looked into his bright green eyes, it felt like a lightning bolt had struck me. It sounds like something out of the movies, but his eyes smoldered as they scanned my face. It was like he was trying to commit every one of my features to memory.

As soon as he asked to sit with me, I knew that talking to him was a bad idea. I had promised myself and my daughter that I was done with relationships and that I was only going to focus on her and nothing else. Connor is exactly the type of man I'd fall for—dirty blonde hair cut short on the sides and the top like a military haircut, chiseled jawline covered in stubble the same color as his hair, muscular build, and the most breathtaking smile.

Thankfully, Love and Jade came to the rescue and stopped me from doing something incredibly stupid, like letting him kiss me.

"Oh, I know what that smile means," Selina chimes in from her spot behind the small reception area, pointing her finger at Love and me.

"How does a smile have a meaning?" I question as we come further into the studio.

"It's all about the reason it's there in the first place." Selina winks at me before turning her attention toward Love. "Does this have anything to do with Jade's dad, Connor?"

"Yes!" Love shouts, throwing her hands up in the air.

"Wait, how did you even know I met him?"

"I didn't, not until you just told me. Now spill, lady. I want to know all the juicy details."

"There's nothing to tell."

"Yeah right, Mom. The two of them were about to burn that whole café down with the way they were looking at each other."

"Ignore her. She's exaggerating things again."

"I don't exaggerate things. I tell them like I see them, and you have the hots for Jade's dad."

"If you want to take some of the amazing classes your Auntie Selina offers here, I suggest you stop talking right now, young lady."

"Oh, you're fighting dirty." Selina snickers, coming from around the desk and wrapping her arm around Love. "Why don't you go into the studio and watch Emersyn practice? I'm sure you can give her some pointers."

"I highly doubt it. But I thought she just worked here?" Love replies.

"She does, but she's been dancing since she was a little girl. It's not something she chose to continue after high school, but you should see her dance. It's beautiful."

"I can't wait to see her," she squeals before stepping out of Selina's arms and heading toward the studio.

"I can't believe Jade and Love hit it off so well. It seems like they have become fast friends," I say, hoping to change the subject.

I know my friends want nothing more than for me to be happy, but right now, I need to focus on Love, not finding love in all the wrong places. If there's one thing I've learned after what happened with Ian, it's that I have horrible taste in men and am probably not the best at judging someone's character. Even after all the warning signs of Ian's secret life, I still foolishly believed that the love we had for each other would solve anything. Man, was I fucking wrong.

"I've never seen Jade open up to someone the way she has with Love. Those two are meant to be the best of friends," Selina says with a smile. "But you know you're not getting out of explaining what just happened with Connor, right?"

"There's nothing to explain." My voice trails off as I grab a brochure from the top of the reception desk, hoping to change the subject. "What class do you think Love should take? She did some pointe classes at her old studio in Texas, but I have to admit, I don't know much about these things."

"Audrey." Selina lets out an exasperated sigh, plopping into a chair beside me.

"Selina," I reply, turning my back toward her, hoping that she drops it, but of course, she doesn't.

"Audrey Serenity Wilde, if you don't stop playing games and talk to me, I'll call Bristol and Leia in for help."

Damn, she means business. I can usually hold out against one of them, but when all three gang up on me, there's no way I'm getting out of telling them whatever they want to know. The only secret I've successfully been able to keep from Selina and Leia is who the father of Bristol's baby is, and that's a secret I'll take to my grave.

"He's gorgeous." I sigh, turning around and resting my elbows on the reception desk.

"Now that's what I'm talking about."

"But nothing can happen between us. He's married and has a daughter who's friends with Love. I can't go there."

After glimpsing his wedding ring sparkling on his left hand, my heart sank. I should have known he had a wife waiting for him to come home. Just my luck. I moved to a new town in another state to start over, and here I am, back at square one, lusting after a married man again.

"Is that your only excuse?" Selina tents her hands in front of her face, her eyes locked on me.

"Excuse? It's not an excuse. I've already been the other woman before, Selina, and I refuse to do that again. I'm not a homewrecker."

"Good thing Connor isn't married. Well, he is, but he also isn't."

My eyebrows pull down in confusion, trying to make sense of what Selina said. "Please explain. How can someone be married and not married at the same time? Is he going through a divorce or something?"

"His wife died during childbirth. So, while he's married and completely devoted to his deceased wife, he is, in fact, single."

"Oh."

"Yeah. He has his parents and all of us, just like you, but he's been raising Jade all alone. She's a good kid, and he's an amazing father, but he doesn't notice women. The fact he noticed you at all is a miracle."

"Thanks for the vote of confidence." I roll my eyes at her before crossing my arms over my chest.

"I don't mean it as a snub." Selina scoffs, "You're gorgeous. Any man would be lucky to have you, but Connor doesn't notice anyone of the opposite sex. Lydia, Connor, and I had been friends since we were younger. They got married after graduation, got pregnant with Jade, and we all thought they'd grow old together, but it seems the universe had other plans."

My heart aches at the thought of losing someone who meant so much to me. I've been searching for that kind of love my entire life and haven't even come close. I used to go to bed every day hoping that the next day I'd find the love of my life, but I've realized that might not be in the cards for me. I have Love, and that's enough. Connor is probably the same way. He lost the only woman he's ever loved and has now devoted himself to raising their daughter.

"We've tried for years to set him up on a date, but he's never taken an interest in anyone. Until today."

"You think he's interested in me?" I scoff, trying to think of any other reason for our awkward conversation in the café. "He was just being neighborly. You are all friends. Of course, he'd make it a point to help me feel welcome."

"Almost kissing someone goes beyond being neighborly," Love chimes in as she comes strolling toward us. "Emersyn is finishing up. It seems like I arrived just in time."

"No one asked you."

"No, they didn't, but I have eyes. The way Connor looked at you meant something."

"Just give it a chance, Audrey." Selina pushes to her feet, throwing her arm over my shoulder and giving it a squeeze. "There's no harm in being nice to someone."

"No, there isn't, but I'm not dating. Not now or ever again. I need to focus on Love. She's entering a very important time in her life, and I need to be there for her, not chasing after some pipe dream of finding true love."

"Don't use me as an excuse, Mom. You always tell me that sometimes you have to kiss a few frogs before you find a prince."

"I've kissed my fair share of frogs. I don't think my prince is ever coming."

"You never know. He might be right in front of you. All you have to do is open your heart," Selina responds without missing a beat.

"I could say the same about you and Vance." I'm fully aware that I should know nothing about her relationship with him, but thanks to Leia, I know some of the details.

"We aren't talking about me or my ex-boyfriend."

"Fair enough, but regardless of Connor's relationship status, I refuse to be a replacement for someone else. Been there, done that."

"Just get to know him, Audrey. See what happens. I promise Connor is nothing like Ian."

"How about we get Love signed up for classes?" I change the subject, not wanting to talk about Connor Bennett any longer. "Thanks again for allowing Love to sit in on a class. Leaving her last studio was hard for both of us."

"No problem. Love is an amazing dancer. She must take after her favorite aunt."

"Already fighting for the favorite aunt title?" I shake my head as Selina hands me a stack of paperwork to fill out.

"I don't have a favorite. Well, unless telling you that you're my favorite aunt is to my advantage." Love pipes in.

"I like the way you think," Emersyn chimes in as she steps behind the reception desk and gives Love a wink. "While your mom fills out the paperwork, let's look at Jade's class schedule and see what classes we have room to slide you into."

"That would be awesome! Having a friend in class would be amazing."

"Jade usually sticks to the ballet classes, but she takes a hip-hop class now and then," Emersyn says as she presses some buttons on the computer and points toward the screen.

Once I finish the mound of paperwork, I hand it back to Selina. "Do you have a recommendation of what classes Love should take?"

"We're flexible about what classes she attends. Based on what Love has told me about her dance experience, she can take any of our classes," Selina says with a soft smile as Emersyn nods her head in agreement.

"I think we have it all figured out." Emersyn presses a few more keys on the keyboard, and the printer comes to life. "Here is a copy of your schedule, Love. If you ever need any help training, getting to class, or anything, just let me know."

She writes something on the top of the sheet before handing it to Love.

"Thanks," Love replies quickly, folding the paper a few times and shoving it into her pocket. "It was nice meeting you, Emersyn."

"The pleasure was all mine. I'll see you in a couple of days when you come in for your next class."

"That's if she doesn't show up here before then." We all laugh as Love's cheeks flush with embarrassment.

"Alright, now that we have that taken care of, let's get you two to your new home." Selina grabs a set of keys off the hook attached to the wall behind the desk.

"It's alright, Selina." I smile, threading my arm

through Love's. "We are just going to head home and turn in early. The movers are coming bright and early tomorrow morning."

Although Leia offered to let us stay at one of her parents' rental cottages, I decided to look for a house to rent instead. With the rental cottages being in the hills outside of Tyson's Creek, it's a little further away than I want to be from work and Love's school. Thankfully, I managed to find an adorable three-bedroom craftsman-style home in a neighborhood close to Bristol's house and only a few blocks away from Selina's parents' house.

"Do you need any help moving things in?" Emersyn asks. "I have a couple of guy friends that will do anything for pizza and beer."

"We also know a certain single father who will probably be more than willing to help you." Selina winks at me, causing my cheeks to turn a matching shade of pink to my daughter's.

"We're fine. Thank you both, but we really should be going."

"Bye, Auntie Selina. Bye, Emersyn."

"Bye, Love. Please don't let your mom overdo it. If you need help with anything, just shoot us a text, and we'll be there with bells on," Selina yells, making sure I hear her.

"Will do. I promise," Love replies as she pulls me toward the door.

I give Selina and Emersyn a wave as we head out and climb into the car, and I plug in the directions for our new home. The robotic voice of the GPS leads us a few miles further into town before we pull into our rental home. I smile. "Here it is. What do you think?"

Love doesn't respond but gives me a small smile before climbing out of the car. I quickly follow and bump our shoulders together. "It won't be so bad. You already have Jade as a friend."

"I like her, Mom. You should see her dance! She looks like one of those prima ballerinas on television," Love whispers.

I hear the longing for a chance to put down roots and thrive in her voice. She has never said it outright, but I'm sure she blames me for our recent move. Who would have thought following your heart would lead you in the wrong direction every time?

"You have always been my number one priority, Love. I know that I've been chasing the idea of being in love and making all the wrong decisions, but I promise, this time will be different," I reply, my heart aching as the words slip through my lips.

"What happened with Ian wasn't your fault, Mom. He was nice to you, to both of us. No one would have known he was keeping secrets." Love places her hand on my shoulder and squeezes before continuing toward the door. "I have a wonderful feeling about this place."

"I do, too." I don't know what the future holds for either of us, but I have to agree with Love. I have a good feeling about this place. I have three friends who have become my family and support Love and me. I have a job

I know I'm going to love. I'll get to witness the birth of my first niece or nephew, and Love has already made a friend. Now, I just need to forget the owner of a certain set of emerald-green eyes, and everything will be perfect.

No matter what Selina says, Connor and I can't be anything more than acquaintances. I'd love to avoid him completely, but that really isn't possible for several reasons. The main one is that our daughters have become fast friends. I'll be polite, but things can't go beyond that, no matter how much either of us might want it to.

I shake the negative thoughts from my mind before following Love to the front door, ready to begin our new adventure. We look around the house and map out where our things will go before heading back to the car. It takes a few trips, but we get the car unloaded and unpack the few items we've brought with us. Although most of the furniture in our old apartment belonged to Ian, I had a few pieces I brought with me when I moved in. Thankfully, I had the forethought to pack our things into a storage unit instead of selling them, and the movers will deliver everything else tomorrow. I'll probably have a few smaller items that I'll need to purchase, but we should be good for a few weeks until I collect my first paycheck.

Once we get the last box unpacked, Love and I collapse onto the couch that was left here. Exhausted from driving a good chunk of the day, we order Chinese food and head to bed early. After a fitful night of sleep, thinking about Connor, I wake up bright and early to wait for the movers to arrive.

I finish my morning routine just as Love comes down the stairs, and there's a knock on the door, signaling the movers' arrival. It only takes a few hours for them to move everything in and be on their way. As one of the movers hands me a clipboard with a stack of papers to sign, my stomach growls loudly.

"Do we unpack now, or should we call Bristol, Leia, and Selina for some help unpacking and then get some pizza?" I ask Love, closing the door behind the last mover as they leave.

"Who are you, and what have you done with my mother?" Love places a hand against my forehead, pretending to check my temperature.

"Haha. Laugh it up, smartass."

"How about we unpack the kitchen and see how we feel? I don't want to deal with you again in the morning without your coffee." We both laugh as we head into the kitchen.

There are boxes on every flat surface, making it almost impossible for you to see how amazing this kitchen is. When Bristol sent me the listing for this rental after I decided to move to Tyson's Creek, this is the room I fell in love with. A large double fridge is tucked into the wall to the right, with a small buffet table right next to it. White shaker cabinets wrap around the wall, separated by a decent-sized window with the sink underneath it. Not the largest kitchen, but one of the nicest I have ever had.

"Let's get to it. Then we can call in reinforcements

and order some pizza." Love gives me a smile before cracking open one box.

As we unpack, my mind drifts back to my conversation with Selina about Connor. She's right. There's nothing wrong with the two of us becoming friends, but I have to make sure it doesn't go beyond that. No matter what Selina said, he was just being nice to the new face he saw in town. Nothing more, nothing less. And that's a good thing because I could easily find myself falling back on old habits if he asked me out on a date. After everything that happened with Ian, I need to focus on Love. No more running around in search of someone to love me.

Love and I spend a few hours unpacking before I text the girls and ask for some help and food. Unpacking on an empty stomach is the worst. After Bristol texts me back with a thumbs-up, I get back to unloading as many boxes as I can before the doorbell rings.

"That must be Bristol with our pizza and reinforcements." I smile as I turn on my heels and head for the door.

"Oh, no, you don't. You keep working. We both know that the moment you sit down, it's all over." Love grabs my shoulder, turning me back toward the open box in front of me. "You keep unpacking, and I'll get the door."

"Fine, but don't eat and walk. I don't want pizza sauce on the carpet."

"I make no promises." She snorts as the sound of the doorbell filters down the hall.

I get back to unpacking before hearing Love gasp loudly in surprise. "Jade! What are you doing here?"

Jade? I cock my head to the side, listening intently for any other hint of what's happening, but when I don't hear anything, I head toward the front door. Connor's daughter, Jade, is standing in the doorway holding a large plate of cookies. Her chocolate-brown hair is braided over her shoulder, and a welcoming smile crosses her face.

"We're neighbors." She turns and motions over her shoulder as I notice Connor standing at the end of the driveway, holding a couple of boxes of pizza.

I wave over her head. "You don't need to stand at the end of the driveway. We were going to order pizza anyway." I give him a shy smile as he comes up the walkway to the front door. An earthly smell envelops my senses as he steps closer. My head tilts back as I look up at him towering over me, flashing him a soft smile before ducking my head. He must be over a foot taller than me.

"Sorry to impose, but Bristol said you were moving into my neighborhood. I figured some pizza and help unpacking would be nice."

"Auntie Bristol phoned a friend instead of coming to help us unpack," Love says to Jade, bumping her shoulder against Jade's as they both laugh loudly.

Connor smiles softly at me before shifting the pizzas to one hand. "Or I could just hand you these pizzas and the plate of chocolate chip cookies Jade spent most of the day making and head home."

I release a shaky breath and take the plate of cookies from Jade. This is a bad idea. This morning, I promised myself that I'd limit as much time as I could with Connor, but here he is, standing on my front porch with pizza and a plate of amazing cookies. Thanking him for the food and sending him on his way is always an option.

"Don't do it," Love whispers softly in my ear, having already figured out what I'd planned on doing. "It's just pizza and dessert. Don't make a big deal out of it."

Don't make a big deal out of it? Easier said than done, but she's right. This doesn't have to be anything more than my incredibly gorgeous neighbor coming over to welcome me to the neighborhood.

"My mom would have my head if I did anything like that." I flash him a shy smile before stepping out of the doorway. "Besides, this is more than enough pizza for all four of us."

Jade and Love fly past me into the kitchen, talking a mile a minute about everything and nothing at the same time. Neither of them bothers to help us bring the food in, as they're off in their own world.

"Those two are going to be trouble," I mutter to myself as I place the plate of cookies on the breakfast buffet and rummage around in the boxes beside me for some paper plates.

"They are, but I'm glad Jade finally found someone she could relate to." Connor's deep baritone echoes through the compact kitchen. I catch a hint of sadness in his voice. "She's lived here all her life, but few people look at her with anything but sadness in their eyes."

"She's a beautiful girl. You and your late wife must be proud of her."

"Ah, you've talked to the girls about us."

"Guilty as charged, but it's not my fault. Once Love told Selina about our encounter in the café, I had no choice. When she smells blood in the water, it's all over." I giggle, hoping to lighten the mood. "I hope I didn't overstep, but I noticed your ring when we met, and..."

"You thought I was a creeper who was hitting on the first beautiful woman he saw, although he had a wife waiting for him at home."

"No. No. That wasn't it at all." My face heats with embarrassment as I try to find the words to explain because that's exactly what I was thinking.

My mouth opens and closes like a fish as I search for the right words, but Connor laughs loudly. The gruff sound of his laughter fills the room, wrapping around me like a warm blanket and immediately calming my nerves.

"Okay, it was like that. I don't have the best of luck with men, and when I noticed the ring on your finger, I imagined the worst about you."

"No worries. I totally understand why you thought that." Connor raises his hand, tucking a piece of hair behind my ear, his fingers brushing gently against my skin. "Besides, Jade asked Bristol all about you when she called, and she was more than happy to tell us all about you."

A warm flutter rips through my entire body as I fight the urge to close my eyes and nuzzle my cheek in his hand. This is why I need to stay far away from Connor. The way he looked at me in the café is the same way he's looking at me right now. His eyes are full of so much emotion and something else. I can see it all playing out right before me. It would be so easy to open my heart to this man. But I know that can't happen. I refuse to be so wrapped up in someone that I ruin both my and Love's lives a second time. This is a fresh start for both of us, and I refuse to do it again.

"Oh." I take a step back, putting some much-needed space between the two of us.

Connor rubs the back of his neck before shoving both of his hands into his pockets. "Don't worry, she didn't tell me anything personal. Just the usual, 'Hurt my friend, and no one will find the body.'"

"That would imply something might happen between the two of us." I giggle nervously, the butterflies picking up speed in the pit of my stomach.

"Yes, it would."

My body shivers as he looks at me. If I don't change the subject quickly, I might do something incredibly stupid, like kiss him. I turn around, shoving my hands into the closest box to keep myself occupied. "Now, where are those plates?"

"I'm sorry. I didn't mean to make you feel uncomfortable. I can just grab Jade and get out of your hair."

"No, please. Stay," I respond breathlessly, my eyes still focused on whatever is inside this box. "My brain is always jumping to conclusions. I doubt you meant anything by what you said, but..." He holds his hand up, halting my words.

"You didn't get the wrong idea, Audrey."

"I'm just not... Love and I have just moved because of a bad relationship, and I just... I'm sorry."

"No problem, Audrey. I get it. This is all new to me, too. I'm not sure what it is about you, but I want—no, need—to get to know you better." Connor has a soft smile on his face as he looks over at the girls. "Just think about it. No pressure."

"O-o-kay," I stutter before giving him another shy smile. "Thanks for bringing over the pizza, but I have a feeling my best friend had a hand in this."

"Guilty as charged. I really live a few blocks down the street, but she told me you tended to overwork yourself and wanted me to stop by and check on you. I understand better than anyone. It's been you and Love against the world for all these years. It's hard to let someone help for fear they will think you're weak or unable to take care of her on your own."

"Exactly." Finally finding the paper plates, I raise them above my head in triumph. "Now, let's eat." I place pizza on plates as we all head for the living room. As I take a seat on the couch, I send up a silent prayer, hoping things are finally working out in my favor.

six

connor

On my way back from the office this morning, I noticed Audrey standing outside, instructing the movers, which reminded me of my promise to Bristol to check on her. I was going to stop right then, but I was worried it'd make her uncomfortable, so I went home.

The moment I stepped into the house, Jade began peppering me with demands, wanting to know when we were going to head to Audrey's so she could see Love. I tried to make excuses, but then Bristol texted me, demanding I bring pizza to Audrey, and the rest was history.

Now, I find myself on the couch, right next to Audrey, which is kicking my senses up to high alert. I should move, find another seat, and put some space between the two of us, but I remain rooted in place. I meant what I said to Audrey in the kitchen. I'm interested in her. I want to get to know her better and see where this connection I feel to her leads. However, she's scared. I saw it when we were talking in the kitchen, so I can't push her, or I'll ruin everything before it has a chance to get started. Right now, my focus is getting to know her and Love. To be her friend, someone she can lean on when she needs help. If things progress to something more than that, so be it.

"This has to be some of the best pizza I've ever had in my life." Audrey moans, her eyes drifting shut as she takes another bite.

My eyes focus on her lips as her tongue peeks from between them, licking them clean. I turn my head to the side quickly, trying to focus on anything else, but the image is playing on repeat in my mind.

"Jesus..." I whisper, causing both girls to giggle softly at the predicament I find myself in. I adjust slightly in my seat, swallowing hard as I try to quell my libido.

"You okay over there, Mr. Bennett?"

"Please, call me Connor. And I'm just fine. You?"

"Peachy keen, Mr. Bennett. Peachy keen."

"Are you sure everything is okay, Connor?" Audrey questions, reaching down and giving my hand a small squeeze.

My eyes snap to hers. Her hair is sitting on the top of her head in a messy bun. A few tendrils fall around her face, her eyes shining with nothing but concern as she pulls her bottom lip between her teeth. My hand moves on its own, brushing my thumb across her bottom lip before pulling it free. Our eyes remain locked on each other, the air crackling with energy as I lean toward her.

"Crap." At the sound of Love's voice, we jump away

from each other as if we'd been burned. Her cheeks are a bright shade of pink as she picks up the paper plate flipped over on her lap. "I'm so clumsy."

"Please continue. Don't mind us." Jade wiggles her fingers in our direction as she grabs a stack of napkins off the makeshift coffee table and hands them to Love.

"I'll grab some more napkins from the kitchen," I push to my feet and hurry into the kitchen. It takes me a few minutes, but I find another stack of napkins and a small rag near the sink.

"You can't hide in here all night. You're gonna have to face the music at some point." Jade comes into the kitchen, grabs the small rag, and runs it under some water.

"I'm not hiding, Squirt." Her green eyes light with fury as she crosses her arms over her chest.

"I've asked you a million times to stop calling me that, old man." She sticks her tongue out at me. "But don't change the subject. You're definitely hiding."

"Okay, you're right. I'm hiding." I chuckle softly before leaning against the counter next to her.

"You like Love's mom, don't you?" She freezes in place; hope fills her eyes as she looks at me.

"You know I do." I sigh loudly, unable to avoid having this conversation any longer. "Does that bother you?"

I'd have loved to get to know Audrey better and see how things went between us before letting the girls know anything, but I don't want to lie to my daughter. It's been the two of us for the last fourteen years. She is my entire world, and adding someone else to that could spell disaster.

I want Audrey. I won't deny my attraction to her, but we both have children to think about. Almost kissing her in front of our two teenage daughters isn't the best idea. Not only could it send her running in the opposite direction, but it could give the girls the wrong idea. Both seem 100 percent on board with Audrey and me being in a relationship, but if things don't work out, what happens? I need to take things slow with Audrey, no matter the pull I feel toward her. This is going to be harder than I expected—complete and utter torture—but deep down, I know there's something between us.

"If I were to start something with Audrey, would you be okay with it?" I hold my breath, waiting for her response "If you have an issue with it at all, I won't do anything. You're my number one priority, no matter what," I reassure her.

Jade rises onto her tiptoes and places a kiss on my cheek. "I'm perfectly fine with it. I'm not a little girl anymore, Dad. I know you love me more than life itself, but it's time to make yourself happy."

"Who said I wasn't happy?"

"No one, but I can see it in the way you look at her."

"How do I look at Audrey?"

"Like she's the missing piece in your life." Jade gives me another kiss on the cheek.

"Okay? That's it? No, *what are you doing, Dad?*

Don't screw this up? Nothing?" I grip her arm, spinning her around to look at me. My eyes scan her face, searching for any hint that she is lying to me, but I find nothing. My little girl really is growing up.

"Nope." Jade shakes her head slightly. "You deserve to be happy, Dad. Mom would want that for both of us."

I pull her in for a one-arm hug before planting a kiss on the top of her head. "When did you get so smart?"

"I've always been smart." She gives me a bright smile before stepping out of my embrace and heading out of the kitchen.

"Did I give you the answer you were looking for?"

"You sure did." I wink at her before following her out of the kitchen and plopping back down on the couch beside Audrey and shoving another bite of pizza into my mouth.

In between mouthfuls, we take turns asking every question we can think of, avoiding anything too heavy. I find out Audrey's favorite color is red, which Jade and Love announce is beyond basic. She loves curling up with a good book next to the fire and hanging at home, watching movies with Love, more than anything else in the world, just like me.

The more we talk and spend time together, the more I let my guard down and show her the real me—the man I was before Lydia died. A man that I forgot even existed until I met her.

"How can *The Princess and the Frog* be your favorite

movie?" Love recoils, as if someone smacked her across the face.

"Because it's an awesome movie!" Jade throws her hand up in the air before turning to me. "Dad, back me up here."

"It is an epic movie," I murmur, shoving another bite of pizza into my mouth, avoiding the need to elaborate further.

"See? It's not my fault. The only people I've had movie nights with were my uncle Vance and my dad."

"I highly doubt that. You're so outgoing. You probably have people lining up to hang out with you on the weekends," Audrey chimes in, running her hand across the back of Jade's head.

"You'd be surprised," Jade huffs, her shoulders sagging slightly. "I like to dance to my own drum, which makes me not so popular with the kids at school."

"The kids at school suck." Love responds immediately.

"You don't even know them." Audrey smiles softly, her attention focused completely on the girls.

"I don't need to. They are mean to you, so they suck." Love throws her arm over Jade's shoulder, pulling her in for a quick hug. "But screw them. You have me now. We can have all the sleepovers and movie nights we want. Right, Mom?"

"Of course." Audrey wraps both girls in her arms. "I'm so glad you two have each other."

"Me, too," I reply, my eyes locked on Audrey.

"And what is your favorite movie, Connor?" she comments, quickly changing the subject.

Jade cackles loudly as Audrey and Love look at her in confusion. "Oh, this is going to be hysterical. Go ahead, Dad. Tell them what your favorite movie is."

"*The Princess and the Frog,*" I say with conviction, watching both girls break out in peals of laughter again.

"I can't believe that's your favorite." Audrey's eyes shine with mirth as she brings the can of soda to her lips.

My eyes lock on her lips as she takes a healthy sip of her soda before licking her lips clean. I shake my head, trying not to continue down this line of thinking, but my eyes remain focused on her as she takes another sip, and the muscles in her neck tighten as she swallows the cold liquid down her throat.

"Don't knock *The Princess and the Frog.* Not only did I have to watch it a million times with Jade when she was younger, but the music is amazing." I chuckle as I grab a pillow off the couch and place it on my lap, trying to cover my desire for her. Slow. We need to take things slow, for both our sakes.

"You're so weird, Dad." Jade rolls her eyes before turning to Love. "See, now is my favorite movie weird?"

"Nope, not at all." Love places her paper plate on the table, holding her hand out to Jade. "Let's ditch these two and head upstairs to my room. Maybe you can help me figure out where to put all my stuff."

"I thought you'd never ask." Jade smiles before turning toward me. "Is that okay?"

"Of course, Squirt." I chuckle as she scowls in my direction before following Love out of the room and up the stairs.

"Alone at last." I chuckle, turning slightly on the couch, causing our knees to brush against each other. Her posture straightens slightly before relaxing, as if she was preparing for me to pounce on her. As her eyes flick to mine, I smile slightly, wanting to put her at ease. "Time to ask some more personal questions."

From the small bits of information I've gotten out of Audrey, she hasn't had the best of luck when it comes to love. She needs someone who's willing to show her how much she means to them, not a man trying to get his dick wet and move on. I know that's not the type of guy I am, but Audrey doesn't know me from Adam. No matter what happens between the two of us, Audrey needs someone she can depend on, and I plan on being that person.

"Have you lived in Tyson's Creek your entire life?" Audrey asks, breaking me from my thoughts.

"What?" I recoil from her question, as if she threw a bucket of ice-cold water on me.

Audrey expects this to be an easy question for me to answer, but that's not the case. I've spent my entire life here with Lydia. The last thing I want to do is make Audrey feel as if she might be a replacement for my wife, but she is a huge part of me. One that I don't plan on forgetting just because I'm interested in another woman.

I want to tell Audrey everything, but I don't want to send her running in the opposite direction.

"I grew up here."

I send up a silent prayer that she'll accept that as an answer, but of course, she won't settle for anything but the entire truth.

"You can talk about your wife, you know. I know you grew up together. No one should expect you to forget about her just because she's no longer here."

"You're very perceptive," I respond, lifting her legs and placing them in my lap. "I just don't want you to think..." My voice trails off, unable to find the right words to explain what I'm thinking.

"That you're looking for someone to be her."

"Yes." I sigh in relief. "I like you, Audrey. Probably more than I should, after only knowing you for a few days, but I will always love my wife. She was my first love, the mother of our daughter, and she will always have a piece of my heart."

"I understand," she replies softly.

"What about you? Why did you decide to move to Tyson's Creek?"

"It's complicated." I can hear the defeat in her voice, but maybe I can use her curiosity to my advantage. Audrey drops her head to her chest. I can tell she doesn't want to explain to me why she suddenly moved her entire life to a small town near the Tennessee-Alabama border, but hopefully, at some point, she will.

I reach forward, lifting her chin with my hand,

forcing her to look me in the eye. "I'm sorry. I never should have asked such a personal question."

"No, it's okay." Audrey pulls her chin from my grasp, turning toward the fire. "Can we just leave it at we needed a fresh start someplace where there are people we know who love us unconditionally?" Her shoulders sag in defeat as she drops her head into her hands.

"I can understand that." I stand, wanting to give her some space, and head toward a group of boxes near the fireplace. "Having family—people who support you unconditionally—is a must when you're all alone. Thankfully, I have my parents and friends who love Jade almost as much as I do. Let's make a deal. If you tell me why you decided to move to Tyson's Creek, I'll tell you what you want to know. All you have to do is ask."

After a few moments of silence, Audrey speaks. "It must be nice." She chuckles darkly, not bothering to raise her head. "Both of my parents died in a car accident a few months short of Love's first birthday. Luckily, Bristol and her family lived a few doors down and took us in, but after they moved, it was just Love and me."

She lifts her head, staring me straight in the eyes as tears trickle down her cheeks. "I've tried so hard to create the best life for Love, but no matter how hard I try, I end up just screwing things up. We moved here because I was so wrapped up in my own head that I didn't notice the writing on the wall. It cost Love almost everything. She's an amazing kid and doesn't deserve to have such a messed-up mom."

My hands tighten into fists, squeezing them shut tightly so I can feel my nails digging into the palms of my hands. Rage courses through my veins, wanting to rip apart whoever made Audrey feel like this. It's hard being a single parent, but it's even harder when it feels like the entire world is against you. I was lucky, but Audrey needs to be reminded that she isn't alone.

"I know we just met, but I can guarantee that you're an amazing mother." I stride toward her, taking a seat beside her on the couch, wrapping my arms around her as painful sobs rack her entire body. "Anyone who spends five minutes with you and Love can see that."

Audrey continues to cry, letting her fear and anger seep into my shirt. I want to tell her that everything will be alright now, but I refuse to lie to her. Being a single parent is hard. Some days are better than others, but we will always doubt the decisions we make and how they affect our children. The only thing I can do for her now is be a shoulder for her to lean on, someone she can talk to with no judgment, hoping one day she'll trust me with all her secrets.

As her tears subside, it's time to give her a little piece of me, as well. "I felt the same way when Lydia died."

She pulls back slightly, tilting her chin up to look me in the eye. "You don't have to do this, Connor. You don't owe me anything. Besides, we just met, and I'm not..."

I place my finger on her lips, silencing her protest. "I want to get to know you, Audrey. I want you to know me and that my love for Lydia is a big part of the man I am today."

I sigh as I tuck a piece of hair behind her ear. "When Lydia died, I was lost. I had no idea how I was going to live the rest of my life without her by my side. But I had this tiny little girl who needed me to take care of her. I didn't know what I was doing, but every day, I woke up determined to be the best father I could ever be.

"I was terrified of making the wrong decisions. Choosing the wrong diapers, deciding when to take her to the doctor, or afraid that if I went to sleep, she'd disappear. But as time went on, it got easier. Sure, I make mistakes, but I've learned to trust myself and my ability to take care of my daughter."

"Do you miss her?" she questions as she slides her hand up my chest, sending shivers down my spine.

"Every day. I'll miss her for the rest of my life, but there's more than enough room in my heart to love someone else." My eyes slip shut as I drop my head to rest on her shoulder, her fingers caressing the small hairs on the back of my neck.

"The pain of losing someone close to you stays with you forever. I'll always miss my parents and wonder if they'd be proud of the woman I've become."

I unwrap her arms from around my neck, clasping them between my hands. "They are. I'm sure of it."

"Gah, I'm sorry to be such a downer. You probably regret coming here." Audrey pulls her hands from my grasp, trying to put some space between us, but I refuse. I place both hands on either side of her waist, lifting her onto my lap.

"I don't. But this isn't the worst date I've been on, not that I've been on a date in the last decade. So I don't have anything else to go on, but it seems pretty amazing if you ask me."

"You thought this was a date?" Audrey questions as she wiggles in my lap, attempting to get away from me, but I tighten my arms around her waist, pulling her to me.

"Do you want it to be a date?" I whisper, brushing my lips against hers softly.

My heart races—no, gallops—in my chest as two emotions swirl through my mind: fear and yearning. Yearning to feel the softness of her golden-brown skin against my calloused fingers. Then, the fear takes hold of my heart, making it feel as if I'm unable to breathe. I know in my heart that there's something here between Audrey and me, but we just met. She moved here for a fresh start, and the last thing she needs is a relationship with a man she just met ruining it. But I'm unable to stop myself, and the need to be near her slowly overwhelms me.

I swipe my thumb across her cheek, her skin feeling like silk beneath my calloused fingers. I stare into her eyes, committing this moment to memory.

"This isn't a good idea," she whispers as I thread my fingers into her curly hair, pulling her closer.

Our lips brush gently against each other a second time,

and I groan. Resting my head against hers, I close my eyes tightly as I fight for control. My mind and body are at war with each other as the magnitude of her words sink in. A possessiveness unlike any other rages through my mind as the desire to make all those horrible feelings that are swirling in her eyes go away. I want to be someone she leans on when she needs help, her support system, anything she needs, and more. But that nagging voice in the back of my head is telling me to slow down, that if things between Audrey and me start getting serious, then it's going to change ours and the girls' lives drastically. If things go wrong with us, it could ruin everything for her. The fresh start she and Love were searching for could go up in smoke.

"Audrey," I groan, clinging to my last thread of control. "There's just something about you that calls to me. That has reignited my once-dormant heart, and I want to explore it."

I lean forward, nibbling on her earlobe before whispering into her ear. "We can go slow. Get to know each other. All you have to do is say yes."

"Yes."

Unable to resist her allure any longer, I lean forward and capture her lips with mine, pulling her tightly to my chest. Audrey moans in pleasure as she rocks her hips back and forth, rubbing herself against me. I nibble and suck at the exposed flesh below her ear. Gripping her hips tightly, I move her body in time with each of my thrusts, bumping her swollen clit with each pass. I lift my hips slightly, rocking back and forth, attempting to get some relief.

"That's it, Audrey. Take what you need from me." I growl as she sucks on her bottom lip before continuing my exploration of her body.

"More, Connor. I need more." The sound of her moaning my name breaks something inside me, and a flood of emotions bubbles to the surface. Audrey gasps in surprise, and I sweep my tongue inside her mouth.

Our pace quickens as she climbs closer and closer to her release until she buries her face in the crook of my neck, biting down hard on my shoulder to muffle her moans to ensure the girls don't hear us. I slow our pace, bringing her down from her orgasm as she snuggles into my chest and her breathing evens out.

"Go on a date with me," I whisper, wrapping my hand around her waist and lifting her off my lap before standing.

"Okay." She responds, her eyes focused on my hand as I adjust my cock in my pants and hold my hand out toward her.

"I should probably go."

Audrey's cheek turns a bright shade of pink as she grasps my hand, and I pull her to her feet. "Yeah, or we might do something we both regret."

"I'll never regret what just happened, Audrey." I bend down and brush a gentle kiss on her lips, stepping back quickly before I deepen the kiss further. "But I heard from a little birdy that you start work this week, and you need to finish unpacking."

"Does that little birdy have red hair and the need to meddle in everyone's business?"

"Maybe, but if she didn't meddle, it probably would have taken me weeks to pull my head out of my ass and ask you to go out with me." I chuckle and call Jade's name, letting her know it's time to go.

"You really want to go out with me?" She questions as the girls barrel down the stairs, snickering loudly.

"Wait, what?" Jade's head swivels back and forth, tugging lightly on Love's shirt. "I think our parents are going out on a date."

"They are?" Love narrows her eyes before stepping between her mom and me.

"Yes," I reply, not moving a muscle.

Love means the world to Audrey. It would only take a few words from her to shut down whatever is happening between us, no matter how drawn we are to each other.

"If that's okay with you, of course."

"Love, my dad is a good guy. Besides, if he hurts your mom, I'll help you hide the body."

"Thanks for the vote of confidence, Squirt."

"You're welcome."

Every muscle in my body tenses, bracing for whatever Love has to say.

"Okay." Love shrugs her shoulders before throwing an arm over Jade's shoulders. "I'll walk you outside. The last thing I want to do is see our parents making out."

"I second that." Jade's nose wrinkles in disgust before she winks at me. Love pulls the door open, motioning for Jade to head outside first before she follows, leaving the door open.

"I guess that's my cue to leave." I chuckle, stepping out the door as Audrey pulls it closed behind her, leaning against it.

"Call me later?" she asks, pulling out her phone and handing it to me.

"Wild horses couldn't stop me." I quickly plug my number into her phone and shoot off a text to myself. "I'll talk to you soon." I smile before planting a kiss on her forehead and heading down the driveway.

seven

connor

The blaring sound of my cell phone pulls me from a very pleasant dream of Audrey's lips pressed against mine in a very passionate kiss. I groan loudly, slapping my hand along the nightstand beside my bed, silencing the alarm on my cell phone. I stare at the ceiling, my mind racing with images of her laid out on the bed beside me. I reach down, squeezing my aching cock, as I imagine what it would feel like to have her body pressed tightly against mine.

Just as I'm about to take matters into my own hands, my phone chimes softly.

I roll to my side, quickly snatching it off the nightstand and unlocking it. A smile spreads across my face as I notice the new message from Audrey.

AUDREY

Good morning! I hope I didn't keep you awake too late last night.

CONNOR

Morning, beautiful. No, you didn't, but the lack of sleep would be worth it.

AUDREY

Charmer.

CONNOR

Only for you.

Audrey and I have texted back and forth over the last couple of days, but that isn't enough for me. I spend most of my days chatting with her, and when I'm not texting her, I'm thinking about her. It's like every minute of my day is filled with nothing but her. I know I said I wanted to take things slow, to take my time getting to know her, but all my plans went out the window the moment we kissed. I've wanted to kiss her since I laid eyes on her in the café. I had planned for it to be a tentative kiss, a quick brush of our lips to take the edge off, but when I placed my lips against hers, my world was set on fire.

CONNOR

Do you have any plans for the day besides unpacking?

AUDREY

Bristol wasn't feeling well today, so I'm going to head in to teach her class this afternoon. Do you think Jade would mind keeping Love company before dance class this afternoon? I can drop them both off.

CONNOR

Do pigs fly? Of course. I'll let her know Love is able to hang out. She's been champing at the bit to come over again. She misses her friend.

AUDREY

We just saw you guys a few days ago.

CONNOR

What can I say? You ladies are memorable. I can drop Jade off on my way to work this morning.

AUDREY

You're the best. Thank you.

I chuckle softly as I throw my legs over the edge of the bed and make my way into the bathroom. I take care of business before quickly hopping into the shower and getting ready for the day, all thoughts of taking my dick in my hands forgotten. Audrey is going to be at Nurture Space today, which gives me the perfect excuse to come see her.

It's almost unnatural how attracted I am to a woman I just met, but there is something about her that keeps drawing me closer to her. Suddenly, I could see a future with her. Lazy afternoons spent cuddling on the couch, watching movies with the girls, family vacations to the coast, quiet nights spent watching the stars and making plans for our future... things that I always imagined I'd be doing with Lydia.

I meant every word I said to her about Lydia. I will always love her, but I'm not looking for someone to replace her. Lydia will forever be a part of the man I've become, but for the first time, I'm able to imagine what my life could look like if I opened my heart to someone else.

After finishing in the shower, I pull on some clothes and make a beeline for Jade's room. I knock loudly, hoping she's already awake, but that would be too much to ask. "Jade. Are you awake?"

"Depends. What do you want?" Jade mutters, no doubt still bundled up in her bed.

"Audrey texted and said Love would like some company today while she's at work." I knock again, hoping to entice her to get out of bed.

I hear a loud thud a few moments before her door flies open. "I require coffee and donuts. I'll be ready in ten minutes."

"Deal. I need to stop and grab some stuff for the guys this morning anyway."

"Bribery gets you everywhere," she comments before slamming the door shut in my face.

I chuckle softly before heading down the stairs. Jade is right about one thing: I'm going to need one hell of a bribe because today seems like the best day to look at the AC unit at Bristol's studio. We are beyond busy, and have been for the past few weeks, but why wait till later in the week when Audrey may not be there? This way, I can kill two birds with one stone.

Now that I've decided to give a relationship with Audrey a try, there's no going back, but I need to tread carefully with her. Audrey fears being hurt and doing something that will jeopardize the new start for her and Love—and probably many other things she hasn't shared with me yet. If I push her too quickly, she's likely to pull away, ending things between us before they have a chance to get started. Not to mention, I also have a teenage daughter to worry about. Love and Jade have become fast friends. I need her to understand that I'm not some asshole who wants a quick fuck, that what's happening between us is bigger and deeper than anything I've felt for anyone other than my wife.

"Okay. I'm ready." Jade comes barreling down the stairs, shoving her pajama-clad legs into her UGG boots that are sitting beside the door.

"Do you plan on putting on clothes? You remember you have dance class later today, right?" I chuckle, grabbing my keys off the hook and pulling the front door open.

"Oh, yeah." She shakes her head and walks back into her room for a few minutes before reappearing with her backpack over her shoulder, pulling her hair up into a messy bun on the top of her head. "Clothes are in the bag for dance and the day. I have no doubt Love is still passed out in bed right now. I have every intention of climbing in right beside her and going back to sleep."

"You really like Love, don't you?" I say, stepping out the door after Jade and pulling it shut behind me.

Jade has never taken to another person as quickly as she has Love and Audrey. She's had a few friends at school and dance, but no one she's really connected with. Jade has always been an old soul, growing up a lot quicker than her peers, choosing to hang out with me and her uncle Vance instead of kids her own age.

"Yes," Jade replies, pulling her door open and climbing inside the vehicle.

I resist the urge to roll my eyes at her as I open my door and climb inside. Trying to get my teenage daughter to talk to me about anything is like pulling teeth. "Are you going to elaborate on that?"

"She gets me." She shrugs her shoulders, turning her head and looking out the window as I pull out of the driveway. We ride in silence for a few moments before she speaks again. "It's only her and her mom, just like you and me. Everyone I know has both parents at home—a mom and a dad. Which is awesome for them, but I don't know..."

"I get it. Sometimes it's nice to have someone that understands all aspects of your life."

"Is that why you like Audrey?"

I recoil slightly at her question, not sure how to answer it. There are a million reasons I might be drawn to Audrey, but none of them I want to discuss with my daughter, at least not yet. "No."

"Are you planning to elaborate?" She turns toward me, crossing her arms over her chest as I pull into Audrey's driveway.

"No."

"How is that fair?" She giggles as I shut off the car and turn toward her.

"Life's not fair, Squirt." I chuckle before pulling her to my side. "But don't get your hopes up about Audrey and me being anything more than friends."

"It will all work out. We have a good feeling about you two." Jade wraps her arms around my waist, hugging me tightly.

"We?"

"Love and me." She shakes her head, as if what she just said was common knowledge. "Did you really think we didn't have an entire conversation about our parents getting together and becoming siblings?"

I open my mouth to respond, but she cuts me off quickly. "Don't be weird about it, Dad." She unwraps her arms from around my waist and opens the door.

"I'm not being weird," I mutter as I climb out of the truck and follow behind her.

Once we get a few steps from the door, it opens, and Audrey steps through it. My breath hitches at the sight of her. A tight pair of pants hug the curves of her hips, and the edge of her shirt pulls up slightly, exposing her flawless, warm brown skin. My eyes trace down the lines of her body before snapping back to her face. Her cheeks flush as a small smile spreads across her face.

"Good morning," she whispers as Jade slides by her and into the house.

"Morning," I reply, as my stomach knots from nerves.

It's as if I've been transported back to high school.

The lanky kid, afraid the girl he's been crushing on for years will reject him. Should I shake her hand, give her a hug, kiss her? My mind is racing with which would be the proper greeting and not cross a line with her. I want to kiss her, my body and mind moving on its own as I lean forward, seconds away from pressing my mouth to hers before a soft giggle reaches my ears.

"I thought you didn't want to watch your parents make out?" I chuckle, standing up straight and taking a step back from Audrey.

"I don't, but you two are just so adorable." Jade rests her head on Love's shoulder as they both stare at us. "Just like in a romance novel."

"Didn't you say something about going back to bed the moment Jade arrived?" Audrey chimes in, narrowing her eyes at our daughters.

"Yes, but that was before Mr. Bennett tried to kiss you."

"Right, who is going to protect your honor if we left, Ms. Wilde?"

"Enough, you two." I groan, reaching my arm up and rubbing the back of my neck.

As if trying to navigate dating for the first time in years wasn't hard enough. Now, I also have to contend with two teenage girls and their snarky comments. I'm sure they mean well, but they aren't helping matters in the slightest. If anything, they're making things even more awkward between Audrey and me.

"Bye, Mr. Bennett," Love says, before threading her

arm through Jade's and pulling her further into the house. "Thanks for bringing Jade over. I promise I'll keep her out of trouble."

"Keep me out of trouble? Who says I won't be keeping *you* out of trouble?"

"Call it my intuition," Love comments, causing both Audrey and me to laugh loudly.

"Bye, Dad," Jade gives me a small wave over her shoulder. "And you still owe me coffee and donuts."

"You two have fun, and please, call me Connor."

"Sorry about that." Audrey grips my arm, giving it a soft squeeze. "After everything that happened before we moved, Love is a little protective."

"As she should be."

Audrey looks down at her hand, realizing she's still touching me, and snatches her hand back.

"I really need to get going. We have a busy day ahead of us, and if I want to get home while it's still light out, I better be going." I smile, tucking a stray piece of hair behind her ear, swallowing down the disappointment that I can't stay here with her.

"Bye, Connor," she replies as I slide through the door, closing it softly behind me.

I make my way back to my truck and make a quick stop at Just the Drip to grab coffee and muffins for the guys before heading to the office. I wasn't kidding when I said I needed to butter them up. I need to get things moving today if I want to get to Bristol's place to repair the air conditioner instead of waiting until later in the week.

It only takes me a few minutes before I pull into my spot in front of the trailer we use as an office and stroll inside.

"Is that for us?" One of the guys mumbles, eyeing the bag of muffins and the carton of coffee in my hand.

"Who else would it be for?" I reply, dropping everything on the table in the break room before heading into the office in search of Vance.

"Did you bring any for me?"

"You have legs. Get up and get your own. But you better hurry before the guys devour it all."

"I'd have thought you'd be in a better mood this morning." Vance raises his eyebrow at me as he leans back in his desk chair.

"I am in a good mood." I chuckle, grabbing my travel coffee mug and striding back into the break room.

"Is there a specific reason for said good mood?" Vance questions from beside me as he fills his own cup with coffee and grabs a muffin.

"Why don't you tell me what you're hinting at so we can get to work?"

"Nothing. Can't a friend inquire about another friend's good mood?"

I ignore his question, head back into our office, and drop into my chair. Vance and I have been friends for years, so I know when he's completely full of shit. He must have talked to one of the girls about what happened between Audrey and me. If I had to guess, I'd say it was Bristol because she loves to meddle almost as much as Vance does. It would be easy for her to poke him for information, not that I have anything to report to either of them right now.

"Where is the schedule for today? I know we have a lumber delivery for the Estates project, but Bristol needs me to repair the new thermostat we installed a few weeks ago."

"I thought you and Jade headed over there to take a look a few days ago?" Vance questions as he drops the schedule for the day onto my desk.

"We stopped by, but I couldn't get it working. I let her know I'd come by later this week and look at the unit, but it's going to be hot. I don't want her to suffer because of a blocked air condenser or a refrigerant leak."

"I knew we should have convinced her to put in an entirely new unit." Vance leans against my desk as he takes a large bite from his muffin. "I can head over and look. I've been meaning to stop in at the dance studio and say hi to Selina anyway."

Living in a small town, we know everything that goes on here. No one leaves or arrives without someone knowing. That is why I know for a fact that Vance has no desire to just say hi to his high school sweetheart. She left without saying goodbye to anyone but Lydia. She headed off to Juilliard and never looked back. Now she's home, and Vance wants answers.

"You sure you don't want to torment her instead?" I

look over the schedule and find two hours where I can squeeze in a visit to Nurture Space. If I'm lucky, things will go quickly, and I can get over there earlier.

"Yup, just like you don't want to go check out Audrey Wilde in her element."

"Is Audrey going to be there today?" I respond quickly, my voice raising slightly, letting Vance know all he needs before pouncing.

"Try that on someone who doesn't know you. From what I hear, she's kinda cute. Maybe I can ask her on a date."

My eyes narrow in his direction as a wave of possessiveness shoots through my body. I know Vance has only ever had eyes for Selina, but thinking about him looking at Audrey sends me into a fit of rage. "Too late. I already did."

"Good on you." Vance pumps his fist in the air. "Are you going to tell me how you grew a set and finally asked the girl you like out on a date?"

I roll my eyes as I move the mouse on my computer, bringing it to life. "I don't kiss and tell."

"So, you kissed her?"

"A gentleman never kisses and tells."

"That would imply that you were a gentleman. Practically celibate since Jade was born, maybe. But a gentleman, you are not." Vance chuckles, slapping me hard on the back.

"Vance."

He holds his hands up in surrender as he backs away

from my desk. "Come on. You knew this was going to happen the minute you said something to Bristol. You haven't so much as looked at a woman since Lydia died, no matter how many times we tried to set you up. This is big news."

"I'm glad my lack of sex life is news to all of you," I grumble as I mindlessly scroll through my unread emails.

Even though I knew this was going to happen the moment he asked about my weekend, I was still caught off guard. Waves of guilt wash over me at the mention of Lydia's name. Lydia is gone and isn't coming back. I know that in my mind, but my heart is another story. The six years I spent with Lydia were magical, and some of the best of my life. It's only natural that I wouldn't be able to find someone to replace her in my life. The pain of losing her will always be a part of me, but since meeting Audrey, that pain has lessened considerably.

"You know I meant nothing by it, man. Who am I to talk? I've been pining after the girl who left town to get away from me."

"Selina didn't leave town to get away from you, Vance." I sigh, turning from my computer and staring at him.

Vance is usually such a happy-go-lucky guy, but ever since Selina left town before graduation, he's changed. Not only did she throw away all the plans they'd made for their future, but she broke his heart. Vance has never moved on, waiting patiently for Selina to come back to him. I thought I was willing to do the same with Lydia, to be thankful for the time we had together, but now that I've met Audrey, for the first time, I'm longing for something more.

"May as well have. Now she's back, and I'm doing everything I can to convince Selina to give me the time of day." The light in his eyes dims slightly before he plasters on another fake smile and begins speaking again. "But enough about me. Let's talk about what's going on with you and Audrey Wilde."

"Nothing is going on, per se. Bristol asked me to help her move something into her new house over the weekend. Jade and Love seem to have really hit it off. I dropped Jade at her place before coming here."

"Hold on a minute. You let Jade stay at their house. Without you there. After just meeting her a few days ago." He ticked off each point with his fingers. "You didn't even let me babysit her until she was almost ten."

"That's because I needed her to babysit you at the same time." I chuckle softly before turning in my chair and focusing on Vance.

"Whatever. So, back to Audrey. When are you taking her out?"

"I'm not sure. We haven't set a specific time or date yet."

"And?" Vance glares at me before crossing his arms over his chest.

"And what? That's all there is to tell."

We stare at each other in silence, both waiting for the

other to speak, but neither of us does. "You feel guilty, don't you?"

I sigh, running my hand through my hair as I try to come up with an answer to his question. "Not guilty, but wrong. Lydia and I planned to spend our lives together, and now she's gone. And here I am, ready to move on with someone else."

"Lydia would want you to be happy. And before you argue with me, you haven't been happy. You are an amazing father, business partner, and friend, but that's making everyone else happy. You are someone outside of those things. Connor Bennett deserves to be happy on his own, with the person he chooses."

"I know that. I do, but..." My voice trails off as I try to make sense of the emotions swirling inside me.

"But you're scared of what will happen if things don't work out between you."

I nod my head at his statement. He isn't wrong, but he isn't completely right either. I've already lost one love in my life and barely survived; I don't know if I could survive heartbreak like that again. I know that I've only known Audrey for a short period, but my feelings for her could rival how I felt about Lydia. She was my best friend. We grew up together, and it was only natural for us to end up in a relationship. But Audrey Wilde blew in here like a summer storm, taking me completely by surprise. If I'm not careful, I could be swept away.

"Being scared is normal, Connor. But if we let fear rule our lives, we will never thrive."

"But Jade and Love, Audrey's daughter, are already thick as thieves. I don't want to ruin that for her."

"Stop using your daughter as an excuse to not pursue this thing with Audrey." Vance clamps his hand on my shoulder, giving it a small squeeze. "Look at Selina and me. We still hang out with friends, can even be in the same room with each other, and she hates my guts."

"She doesn't hate your guts, Vance."

"Semantics." He waves away my statement with his hand before heading toward his desk on the other side of the small room and taking a seat. "All I'm saying is if things don't work out, then they don't work out. Love and Jade can still be the best of friends, and then I can ask out Audrey in hopes of making Selina jealous." I pick up a stack of Post-it Notes on the edge of my desk and throw it at him, causing him to laugh loudly. "Okay, maybe that was a step too far."

"Only a little." I shake my head at his antics.

Vance is right. I haven't been living my life to the fullest since Lydia passed away. I've been so focused on growing our business and ensuring Jade's happiness that I haven't thought much about my own. I can be all the things Vance listed and still be an individual of my own. I can have wants and needs that go beyond ensuring that everyone else in my life is thriving. And right now, what I want more than anything is Audrey Wilde.

"Thanks for the pep talk."

"Anytime. Now, we need to get some work done so you can head over to Bristol's and see your girl."

"She isn't my girl, per se. She agreed to go on a date with me, that's it."

"Semantics, my friend. The date is just a formality. If she didn't want to be your girl, she'd never have agreed to go on a date with you." Vance winks before we both turn towards our computers and get to work.

Luckily, the day goes off without a hitch, and I make it to the yoga studio in plenty of time. I don't see any classes going on in the main room through the large window in the front, or anyone standing at the front desk. I know Audrey is covering Bristol's class today, so I'm sure I'll run into her at some point, but I was hoping it would be without an audience.

The small bell on the front door rings as I walk through, and I head toward the back, where the AC unit is located. I look around quickly, wondering where Audrey is, and notice one of the smaller room's doors is closed. She must be teaching a class. I head toward the break room, slightly disappointed I won't see her, but hopefully, we can bump into each other soon.

I quickly get to work checking the air condenser, which is indeed covered in grime, and get to work clearing it out before heading to check the new ducts we installed with the thermostat for any issues. I begin in the front of the studio, placing the ladder within view of the small room where Audrey is teaching to ensure everyone can see the ladder. Once it is locked into place, I climb it quickly and remove the drop ceiling, poking my head inside and using a flashlight to look around.

After a few moments of searching, I find nothing, so I pull the tile back into place and move the ladder. Once I have the ladder locked, I begin the process over again. After a few seconds, I feel something bump into the ladder, causing it to wobble beneath me. I attempt to regain my balance, but the ladder falls out from under my feet. I grasp onto the ceiling support, but unfortunately, it holds no weight, and I come crashing to the ground, landing flat on my back. I clench my eyes shut and try desperately to hold back the groan of pain, wanting to escape.

Once I regain some of my composure, I open my eyes and see Audrey with a shocked expression on her face as she mumbles, "Sorry."

eight

audrey

I take a moment to regain my composure before I bend down to help Connor stand. What a great way to make a good impression on someone.

"Fancy meeting you here," Connor chokes out before clenching his eyes closed tightly and groaning again.

My hand brushes along the side of his face and cups his cheek. Connor nuzzles his cheek into my palm. His eyes are full of pain, but there's something else there, too.

I know this isn't the time for this, but I can't help but notice how beautiful he is. Most men want to be called rugged, handsome, or some other manly descriptor, but Connor Bennett is beautiful, and judging by the way the ladies from my class are simpering behind me, I'm not the only one who thinks so. He's tall, handsome, and has muscles stacked on top of each other. Intricate tattoos run down both of his muscular arms, peeking out from beneath the fitted black T-shirt he's wearing with the Ace & Hammer logo on his chest. After talking to Connor via text and phone over the last few days, I know he has a warm heart and loves his daughter more than anyone in this world. He wears his emotions on his sleeve for everyone to see, unlike other people. You know what you get when you interact with Connor, a quality I admire, especially after what happened with Ian.

"Are you alright?" I ask. My eyes scan his body, searching for any signs that he's injured.

When he doesn't answer me, I lie on the floor beside him, inching my lips close to his ear. "Connor, can you hear me?" I whisper as he lets out a whoosh of air, a shiver running through his entire body, causing a loud groan to leave his lips. My core tightens at the sound, wishing we were anywhere but in the middle of the yoga studio.

Down, girl! This is not the time to climb him like a tree.

"How could you have missed the enormous ladder right in front of you?" Connor asks, turning his head to make eye contact with me.

"I was talking to someone as we left class and ran right into it. Besides, who puts a ladder in front of a door anyway?" I respond defensively, before softening my tone immediately. "I'm sorry. I'm just worried about you."

"No need to worry, beautiful. Just got the wind knocked out of me." He smiles as he rolls to the opposite side, pushing himself up on all fours, giving everyone a marvelous view of his ass. "I just need a minute to catch my breath."

A few of the ladies in the main room bend slightly to

check him out. I don't blame them. If I am being honest with myself, I'm jealous. He was kissing me a few nights ago and texting me every night before bed. *He's mine.*

What? My eyes widen in surprise at my own thoughts. It seems my conversation with Bristol and my subsequent card readings the other night had a bigger impact on me than I thought. Connor is a nice guy with an amazing ass, but this is a fresh start for me. I need to make better choices and learn to make decisions based on what's best for my daughter.

But you agreed to go on a date with him.

So? We've been talking for days, and he hasn't mentioned the kiss or our date once. If he was really interested in me, he'd be champing at the bit to go out with me, wouldn't he? When I met Ian, he was persistent without being pushy. He did everything he could to ensure I didn't forget that he wanted something more from me than friendship. The exact opposite of Connor. Sure, he kissed me, and we've engaged in some light flirting over the past few days, but he hasn't made a move for something more.

Connor isn't Ian.

I'm fully aware of that fact in more ways than one. Ian was always nice to Love and never made her feel unwelcome, even going as far as choosing to stay in instead of going out on dates to include her. However, in hindsight, I doubt he did it out of the kindness of his heart. We were his dirty little secret, the last thing he needed was word getting back to his wife about the other woman he was hiding. Connor asked me out and then immediately asked my daughter's permission. There's no doubt in my mind that if Love had told him he couldn't date me, he'd have been disappointed but would have respected her decision.

"Can I get a little help, beautiful?" Connor groans, bringing me back to the present.

My eyes lock on his body as he sways from left to right, making it clear that there is something very wrong with him. He shakes his head a few times before reaching his hand toward me.

"We need to get you to the hospital." I push to my feet and head toward him, gripping his arm to help him stand. He sways again, his large body leaning against mine for support. It takes a few tries, but I get him to his feet.

"The closest hospital is about twenty minutes away. It's nothing serious. I should be fine after some painkillers and ice." Connor groans loudly as I wrap his arm around my shoulders and move slowly toward the door.

"Nonsense! You more than likely have a concussion, but who knows what else could be wrong? I doubt you broke anything important, but better safe than sorry. I'm taking you, and that's final."

Connor's green eyes blaze as he pulls his arm from my grasp, standing to his full height. "I said I was fine, Audrey."

"And if Jade would have fallen like that? Would you

let her go home without seeing a doctor?" A few of the ladies snicker at his expense.

"She's got you there. You made Jade go to the hospital for a splinter when she was six. You swore it would get infected, and they'd have to cut her finger off," Mrs. Johnson, a woman in my class, chimes in from beside me.

"See! We're going. Luckily, I'm finished for the day." I turn toward the ladies in my class. "Can one of you give Bristol a call and let her know that I'm taking Connor to the hospital?"

"No problem, Audrey. Now, you go take care of your man."

"He isn't..." I begin but decide against it. I've learned that fighting with the old ladies in my seniors' yoga class is a losing battle. The moment I stepped into class, they knew everything there was to know about me and then some. "Thank you."

"You help Connor to your car, and I'll grab your bag from the back." Mrs. Johnson gives my shoulder a squeeze before heading toward the break room.

"We need to find someone to grab the girls after dance class. If we're going to the emergency room, there's no way we'll be back in time."

I pull my bottom lip between my teeth, trying to figure out what to do here. I could call Bristol to grab Love from class, but she isn't feeling well. I'm sure the last thing she wants to do is get out of bed to come get Love.

Leia is out of town for a business meeting, so she is out. Selina would probably hang out with her for a little while after class, but I'm not sure how long we will be in the emergency room.

"I can see the wheels turning in your head. I'll call Vance and ask him to grab both girls from class. He can bring them back to my house until we get back."

"Vance? As in Selina's Vance?" I question as I shuffle him toward the door. "That doesn't seem like a good idea."

"Selina and Vance need a push in the right direction. Jade and Love are exactly what the two of them need," Mrs. Johnson says as she heads for the door, holding it open as I help Connor outside to my car. "As soon as I get you two on your way, I'll head over to Selina's and let her know what's going on."

"Selina will never forgive us for unleashing Vance on her," Connor mutters as we amble toward my car.

"It's easier to ask for forgiveness than to ask for permission."

"I don't know if I'll even fit in that thing," Connor complains.

"You'll fit, don't worry. You aren't that tall." Mrs. Johnson clicks the unlock button on my key fob before opening the passenger-side door for Connor. It takes a few minutes, but I get him inside and his seat belt buckled. As I stand up and shut the door, I stifle a snort. Connor was right. He looks like a sardine stuffed inside my Kia Optima. I give Mrs. Johnson a quick hug as she hands me my bag, and I promise to call to let her know when we find out what is going on before hopping into the car myself.

"I told you I wouldn't fit." Connor moves slightly, attempting to get comfortable.

"You fit. If you push the seat back some, maybe it will be a little more comfortable." I pull out my phone and shoot Love a text, letting her know about the change of plans before asking Connor for directions.

"Just head down Main Street to find the entrance to the highway. There are signs telling you where to go from there."

"How about I just look up the address and plug it into my GPS? I can get lost in a brown paper bag if I'm not careful."

"Why doesn't that surprise me?" Connor holds his hand out for my phone. I reluctantly hand it to him before putting the car in reverse and heading down Main Street, toward the highway.

The electronic voice from my GPS fills the car, alerting me I need to turn around. My cheeks pink in embarrassment as Connor's chest rumbles with laughter. Thankfully, he keeps his comments to himself, and I make a U-turn.

We make it out of town and onto the highway without any more problems before my phone chimes with a text from Love. "Can you check that for me?" I ask as I concentrate on the road ahead of me.

"*Way to go, Mom. Now you can nurse him back to*

health." Connor reads the message aloud. Of course, Love would choose right now to send me a message like that. She has been talking nonstop about my upcoming date with Connor for the last few days. I can only imagine all the fake scenarios she's plotting as we speak.

"Are you planning to be my nursemaid?" Connor questions as he puts my phone back into the holder on the dashboard. "Audrey, there's no need for you to take care of me. They will probably give me some painkillers and tell me to rest for a few days. I can manage on my own."

I ignore his statement and continue driving. There's no way I will elaborate on anything Love has to say. I know my girl; her mind instantly went to Connor and me having babies and living happily ever after. She has a good head on her shoulders, but ever since Connor and Jade have come into her lives, I've noticed a shift. She gone from being her practical pragmatic self, to being more of a hopeless romantic, just like me. However, I doubt she would ignore her common sense in favor of someone who said they loved her, which is the exact opposite of me.

I am insanely attracted to Connor, but I promised myself that I was going to focus on Love. Any relationship I could have with Connor is the least of my concerns right now. Just because we got carried away a few nights ago doesn't mean anything. He isn't interested in being anything more than my friend, no matter how much I'd prefer something more. Right now, my focus needs to be getting settled into our new life here and my daughter. I refuse to fall head over heels for the first guy I find attractive—again. I doubt it would lead to anything other than heartache.

"Why is it so hard to let me help you?"

"I'm sorry, Audrey." Connor sighs. "I've been taking care of myself and Jade for the last fourteen years, and it's been hard for me to ask for help. I have my parents and some friends to help in emergencies, but it's always been just Jade and me."

"I've been alone with Love her entire life, too. There's nothing wrong with asking for help when you need it, Connor. Unfortunately for you, I won't be taking no for an answer. If you need to rest, I will make sure you get it. Besides, the whole reason you fell is because I wasn't looking where I was going."

He chuckles, leaning his head back on the seat. "So bossy."

"I'm a mom. It's part of my DNA at this point." I sigh, glancing at him out of the corner of my eye. "I'm sorry if this is annoying you, but if you don't let me at least make sure you're okay, I'll worry. And me worried is not a sight to behold. Ask Love. She'll be begging you to let me help you in some way."

"That bad, huh?"

"Whatever you're thinking, it's worse."

"Okay. I give up. You can nurse me back to health."

"I'm glad you're starting to see it my way." I snicker softly.

"This isn't what I had in mind when I came to the studio today. I planned on finally setting up our date."

"Our date?"

"Yes, our date. You said you'd go out with me when I came over with pizza and cookies." His voice drops slightly as he turns his attention out the window. "Did you change your mind?"

"No. I didn't change my mind," I rebut, my hands tightening on the steering wheel. "I thought you were just being nice after getting caught kissing me by the girls. If you really wanted to go on a date with me, I assumed you'd have brought it up during one of our many phone conversations."

"I'm a fucking idiot and completely out of practice when it comes to dating women." He reaches across the console, wrapping his large hand around mine. "I was waiting for you to say something. I didn't want to come on too strong or scare you away."

"Oh," I reply, turning over my hand and threading my fingers through his. "I thought you regretted the kiss we shared and only asked me out to be nice."

"First thing you need to know about me is that I don't do anything I don't want to do. I kissed you because it was the only thing I'd wanted since I saw you in Just the Drip. I asked you out because the thought of not spending any more time with you made my heart ache. I even cleared my schedule for today to find a way to get over to the studio so I could see you."

"You don't have to say—wait, what?" I pause, my

head snapping in his direction as the car swerves off the road. The rumbling sound of the strips of uneven pavement on the side of the road fills the inside of my car as I pull over to stop. "You wanted to kiss me the first time you saw me?"

"Yes," he responds without hesitation.

"But… this makes no sense at all."

"It makes perfect sense to me. I haven't been attracted to a woman since my wife died. People have tried to set me up on dates with perfectly acceptable women, but none of them held a candle to you, Audrey."

Audrey shakes her head, ignoring my statement, as she pulls back onto the highway. Her attention remains focused on the road.

"Just let me take you out on a date. Just the two of us, so we can see what this is between us. That's all I'm asking for; a chance to explore this connection between us. There's a chance that we go out and realize this is nothing more than a passing attraction, but deep down in my soul, I know this is more than that. This is the start of something that could change both of our lives forever."

"I promised Love I wouldn't do this. I was going to stay focused on creating a home for us here and on her happiness. I've spent so many years chasing after men and begging them to love me, and after what happened with Ian, I can't even trust my instincts anymore.

I don't know anything about you other than you have a daughter and your wife died during childbirth, Connor.

I knew my last boyfriend for over a year and still ended up with my heart broken."

"What happened between you two?"

I freeze, my eyes filling with tears at the thought of telling someone else about my stupidity. What happened with Ian was completely my fault. Sure, he was a lying, cheating asshole, but the signs were there if only I had opened my eyes.

"Let's just say I had a hard time reading the writing on the wall."

"He's a fucking idiot."

I shake my head, chuckling darkly as my phone instructs me to take the next exit off the highway. "I'm the idiot."

"Anyone who threw away a chance to be with you and Love is an idiot," he replies with conviction, bringing my hand to his lips and kissing it softly. "Remind me to send him a thank-you card. His loss is my gain."

"You're incorrigible."

"You have no idea." Connor laughs loudly and groans in pain at the same time. "Fuck, that hurts."

"Serves you right," I grumble, as the hospital comes into view.

"How about dinner, just the two of us, as friends?"

"Maybe. Can I think about it?"

"I can live with that. If you promise to really think about it."

"I promise. Now, be a good boy, and don't give me a hard time about sitting here with you until they give you a clean bill of health," I respond quickly, trying to change the subject. "I'll even bake you a chocolate cake."

"Deal," he says as I pull into a parking spot and shut off the car, "but you have to let me at least cook for you and Love dinner one night. I'm not the best cook in the world, but I can grill with the best of them."

"I can live with that." I give him a shy smile before opening my door.

nine

connor

After my conversation with Audrey in the car, I knew Audrey wasn't going to drop me off at the emergency room and disappear. She stayed with me, waiting in the emergency room waiting area until my name was called, insisted on being allowed in the room with me, even though she wasn't family, and fussed over me ever since I sat down in this bed. If this was a few weeks ago, I wouldn't have been sitting here quietly, listening to her fuss at me, but if I'm being honest with myself, this is nice.

While we wait, Audrey has talked about anything she can think of to help keep my mind off the pain. I learned about her hippie parents and all the places she's lived over the years. No mention of a boyfriend or Love's dad being in the picture. I take that as a good sign.

Every brush of her hand or touch on my arm sends my body into overdrive. For the last few hours, I've been in constant war with my body, trying to think of anything that could divert my attention and stop my body's reaction to her touch, but nothing has worked.

"Are you sure you're comfortable? It feels a little chilly in here. Do you want another blanket?" Audrey pushes to her feet, poking her head out the curtain, no doubt searching for a nurse to bother.

"I'm fine, beautiful." I shake my head in her direction, wincing slightly as I attempt to get comfortable. "The doctor should be here any minute. He'll tell you I'm fine, and then you'll be off the hook."

"I already told you I'm not going anywhere." She spins on her heels, puts her hands on her hips, and scowls at me. "It's my fault you're here. The least I can do is take care of you."

"Is that the only reason you're here?" I question, not sure I really want to know the answer.

I poured my heart out to Audrey on the way here, letting her know exactly how she made me feel, and her only response was, 'Oh.' Not the biggest confidence boost, if you ask me. When she told me she'd been in a bad relationship recently, I stopped pushing. No matter how badly I want to explore things between Audrey and me, it's obvious she still carries the scars from that relationship. I'm going to need to chip away at the walls she has around her heart, little by little. And the quickest way to do that is to show her I'm not like that asshole who broke her heart. I'll be her friend and let things happen naturally. It's not any different from what I originally had planned, just without the labels.

"Of course not," she snaps. "I..."

"You what?" I poke, wanting to hear how she feels about me.

"I like you, okay. Way more than I should for a man I just met." She huffs, her cheeks turning a delicious shade of pink as she plops down into a seat beside my bed. "But don't get any ideas. We're just friends."

"Friends." I smile, reaching out and brushing a piece of hair from her cheek. "For now."

"You never quit, do you?" She shakes her head, a soft smile on her face.

Just as I open my mouth to respond, the doctor comes strolling in. Audrey listens to each one of the doctor's instructions, asking questions about how much moving around I'm allowed to do. Thankfully, there's nothing seriously wrong with me. My X-rays look fine, and there's no sign of a concussion, but the doctor wants me to rest for a few days.

"You won't try and get rid of me again?" Audrey asks as we slowly make our way back to her car.

"Nope. Just remember, you promised me a chocolate cake for behaving."

"They say the way to a man's heart is through his stomach," she says, barely loud enough for me to hear, as she unlocks the car and climbs in.

We drive back to Tyson's Creek in relative silence, the soft music coming from the radio playing in the background. Thanks to the painkillers the doctor gave me before we left, the ride home is a lot more comfortable than the ride there. Just as I'm drifting off to sleep, we pull into my driveway.

"Thanks for taking me to the emergency room, even though I'm fine."

"You aren't fine, Connor. But you don't have anything majorly wrong with you, which is a good sign." She wags her finger at me before climbing out of the car. "Now, don't move so I can help you climb out of the car." She slams the door closed, effectively ending our conversation.

Audrey helps me get out of the car, with only a few twinges of pain, before my front door flies open, and two very distraught teenagers come flying out.

"Daddy!" Jade shouts, Love right on her heels. "Are you okay? What hurts? How did you fall off a ladder? You're always so careful."

"He may have been a little preoccupied at the time." Love's eyes flicking between her mother and me. "I'm glad you're okay, Mr. Ben—I mean, Connor."

"Thanks, Love. Me, too."

Love wraps her arm around Jade's shoulder, giving her a small squeeze. Jade's entire body seems to sag in relief. It's as if that small sign of support from Love has leeched all the worry for me from her bones. Something that I've never been able to do for her. Who knew that one girl and her mom moving to town could change our lives so drastically in a matter of days?

"Thanks, and thanks for stopping this one from

freaking out too badly." I chuckle as Audrey comes to a stop in front of them.

Jade's hands flail around, unsure where to touch me or what to do with her hands. It seems odd, but this is the first time she's had to deal with anything wrong with me. I've taken her to the hospital for broken bones, fevers, and splinters, but she's never had to deal with something wrong with me.

"He's fine, honey. I made sure of it." Audrey winks at Jade before reaching for her hand and squeezing it. "Now, let's get your dad inside and settled on the couch. Then we can figure out something for dinner."

"Yeah, dinner. I could eat," I reply, sending up a silent prayer of thanks for Audrey and Love.

This is what has been missing. I've always been the one to take care of Jade, but besides the few people I allow to help in an emergency, there's no one to take care of me. The way Audrey and Love have fit seamlessly into our lives is both amazing and terrifying. I can see the four of us forming a family unit, us against the world, but I can also see how heartbroken we would all be if things didn't work out.

"Of course." Jade turns on her heels and scurries back into the house, holding the door open for us as I make my way inside. "Uncle Vance and Selina dropped us off. They wanted to stay and wait with us, but I told him they'd be in the way."

"Good call kicking him out. The last thing I need is him making jokes about me being old."

"You're not going to be able to avoid him for long." Jade giggles softly as she closes the door behind her.

"Your dad won't be doing anything but sitting on this couch and resting for the next few days. Doctor's orders."

"Good luck with that, Audrey. My dad doesn't know what it means to relax."

"He promised to be a good boy and listen to the doctor's orders. Didn't you, Connor?"

"*Good boy*?" Jade raises an eyebrow as we enter the living room. "What are you, three, Dad?"

"What can I say? She promised me a treat if I behaved," I respond, winking at the two girls.

"How about baked chicken and vegetables for dinner?" Audrey says, quickly changing the subject as she helps me sit on my couch.

Love and Jade both prop up pillows to make it a little more comfortable for me to sit down. I don't need all these ladies fussing over me, but I won't complain. It's nice to have someone worrying about me for a change.

Audrey sits down gently beside me and begins rubbing small circles on my back. *This is not helping, lady.* I inhale deeply and hold my breath, praying the lack of oxygen will help tame the beast in my pants.

"Sounds amazing. I can't remember the last time we ate something that didn't come off the grill or from the local diner," Jade chimes in as she bends down to take off my work boots. I lean forward, groaning in pain as I use my forearms to cover the problem in my pants. I don't want to traumatize my daughter.

"You never complained about my cooking before now, Squirt." I bend down further to untie my boots, wincing slightly at the movement.

Jade slaps my hand lightly before squinting her eyes at me. "I asked you not to call me that! Besides, I don't hate your cooking, but sometimes I'd like a home-cooked meal that doesn't come from Grandma's house."

I open my mouth to respond, but she tugs on my leg, sending a jolt of pain up my back. "I'm not complaining, Daddy. You're the best dad a girl could ever ask for, but we all have limitations. Yours is cooking." All the girls cackle as I lean back carefully, replacing my arm with a throw pillow.

I have to bite back a groan as it comes in contact with my aching cock. "Fine. I guess I need to find a cooking class."

Audrey lays a hand on my shoulder as she stands. "I can help. It has been a lot of trial and error, but I can show you a few simple things to make."

"Yeah, Mom wasn't always the best cook. I'm thankful for the cooking network, or we'd probably eat a lot of takeout, too," Love says as she wraps her arm around Jade's shoulder.

Having finally pulled both my boots off, Jade and Love scurry up the stairs to her room as I slowly put my legs up on the couch. Audrey leans down slightly, giving me the perfect view of her breasts through the dip in her shirt as she continues fussing over me. She fluffs pillows and makes sure the TV remote is close enough.

Anything she can think of to make me more comfortable.

"I'm okay, Audrey." I grip her wrist lightly, giving it a squeeze. "Why don't you sit down and relax for a few minutes? You've had a long day, too."

"You're kidding, right?" She continues fussing over me as my eyes drift down to the soft mounds peeking through the top of her bra. "I knock you off a ladder and you're worried about how I'm doing?"

"I can't seem to do anything but worry about you," I mumble as images of her pert nipples filter through my mind. Her smell envelops my senses, and I inhale deeply, lavender and vanilla swirling through my mind. I want to lean forward, bury my nose in her hair, and inhale her scent.

"Are you comfortable?" Audrey places her tiny hand on my forehead. "You look a little flushed."

"As comfortable as I will get." Audrey smiles before cupping my face in her hands, my cock hardening further at her touch. "Thanks for the help."

Audrey heads toward the kitchen. "It's not a problem. I'll get started on dinner. Holler if you need anything."

"Will do." I groan as I move my legs off the couch, my cock pushing against the zipper of my jeans, begging for release.

"You better not be moving around in there," Audrey yells from the kitchen.

"I'm not about to sit here and piss myself, Audrey.

I'm heading to the bathroom. No need to worry. Just focus on whatever you're doing in there. I'll be fine."

The journey to the bathroom has never been more difficult. I am not entirely sure what's worse, the shooting pain running down my legs as I make my way to the door or trying to move with my cock as hard as a rock.

After what feels like an eternity, I fling the bathroom door open and brace my arms on the sink. I try to think of anything other than bending Audrey over my kitchen table and fucking her senseless. "This is not helping." I groan as my hand grips my cock, begging for some relief.

Suddenly, I remember I left the bathroom door open and turn to my right, pulling the door shut. The last thing I need is someone walking by and catching me with my dick in my hands while I'm trying to go to the bathroom. There will be no living with Jade if that happens.

I make my way over to the toilet, unzip my jeans, and my cock springs free. I grip it tightly in my hand, pumping my fist up and down a few times to relieve the pressure, to no avail.

"Go to the bathroom and put your dick back in your pants. You're a grown-ass man. There's no way you're rubbing one out in your guest bathroom like a teenage boy."

If I say it out loud, I can make it so, right? Isn't that the saying? But no amount of willpower can stop the image of Audrey's perfect breasts waiting for me to pull them between my lips. Thankfully, I make quick work of going to the bathroom before stuffing my cock back into my pants and heading back to the sink to wash my hands. I close my eyes, focusing on the task at hand as my mind wanders.

Images of her beautiful eyes, full of need, as she spreads her legs from me. She lifts her leg over the arm of the couch, giving me the perfect view of her pussy and the insides of her thighs coated with her juices.

I groan loudly, squeezing my cock tightly in my hand. My hand pumps up and down my shaft slowly, gathering the pre-cum leaking from my tip and using it to lubricate my movements.

"Connor," she moans as her slender fingers slip between her folds.

I groan again, louder this time, pulling my hand faster up and down my shaft. My eyes focus on her fingers disappearing between her folds. My mouth waters at the thought of tasting her skin, and I step forward, pulling her taut nipple into my mouth.

"Fuck me. Please," she begs, as I wrap her legs around my waist, slowly pushing my cock inside her, not caring if we're caught by our girls.

Lifting her shirt over her head, I give the opposite nipple the same attention as I thrust my hips into her warm center. My cock hardens even further as the tip hits her sensitive bud before sinking into her.

"That's right, baby. I can't wait to feel your juices dripping down my cock," I thrust my hips forward and sinking deeper inside her. Pain shoots through my back and legs as I

pump my hips faster, climbing higher toward oblivion. Her eyes fill with passion as she begs me to let her come.

"Come for me, Audrey. I want to see you come undone. Come all over my cock like a good little girl." I growl as I slam my hips home. Blinding white light fills my vision as I collapse on top of her.

"Connor!" she screams before biting down on my shoulder, trying to keep our actions a secret from everyone in the house. My knees buckle from the pleasure coursing through my body, and I collapse on top of her.

"Dad, time for dinner," Jade shouts as she bangs on the bathroom door, bringing me back to the present.

I startle slightly, pain shooting up my back as I grip the side of the sink. "Be right out," I reply through clenched teeth before washing my hands quickly.

"Teenage boys have it much easier," I say to my reflection before flicking off the light and heading toward the kitchen.

ten
audrey

Dinner is a hit. Both girls clean their plates in no time before heading back upstairs. I make sure Connor is settled on the couch before I begin the dishes. Connor tried to take care of them, but there was no way I would let him stand there washing dishes, especially after being the reason he was hurt. I wince slightly every time I see him struggle to move around the house or give his daughter a hug. He keeps telling me it was an accident, and I know that, but all my mind can focus on is how much worse things could've been.

If I knew what was good for me, I'd have just dropped him off here, grabbed Love, and headed home. But a small part of me enjoys being here with him and Jade, taking care of them as if the four of us are one big, happy family. I can see a future here with the four of us, spending lazy Sundays huddled together on the couch, watching movies, and having family game nights and large dinners with all our friends. Creating a home full of happiness and love, something that Love and I have been missing for some time now.

But I need to be careful. On the surface, Connor seems like my ideal man: gorgeous, with his own house and business, and I can already tell that he's beginning to care for my daughter, as well. Things weren't much different with Ian in the beginning, but we know how that turned out. Although Connor has said we could just be friends, he's made it more than clear that he can see there is something more between us. Hell, so can I, but I promised Love this time would be different. It's time for me to focus on my daughter and her happiness.

People say that men and women can't be friends, but it's happened in the past. Now all I need to do is get control of my libido. Friends don't sleep with each other, at least the type of friends I should be with Connor, that is. Just being in the same room is almost unbearable. I can't stop thinking about how his body felt pressed against mine, how his eyes drifted shut, and the hum of contentment that passed his lips every time I touched him.

"Hey, Audrey. Do you need any help?" Jade's voice is like a bucket of ice water being dumped on all my fantasies.

"Since I don't know where anything goes, can you put the dishes away? I'll wash, and Love can dry."

"You got it," Jade says with a smile before grabbing a dish towel from the drawer.

"Hey, Love, get your booty in here so we can get these dishes finished!" I shout, knowing she's lurking nearby.

"No need to shout, Mom. I'm standing right here," Love mutters as she grabs the dish towel from Jade and gets to work drying the dishes.

The three of us work in silence before Jade blurts out, "Thanks for taking care of my dad."

"It's the least I could do. After all, it was my fault," I respond with a smile, my attention focused on the dishes.

"No, Audrey. Taking him to the hospital and making sure he won't sue you is what any normal person would've done," Jade mutters. "But you made sure he was okay. You made sure there was someone there to take care of me, and you made sure that I wouldn't be left here alone."

"Your dad..."

"My dad probably told you nothing was wrong and tried to go on as if nothing happened, but you made him get looked at," Jade rebuts, her voice thick with emotion. "My dad is the strongest person I know, but it's nice to have someone looking out for the both of us for a change."

I freeze in place, wondering exactly what the right thing to say is at this moment. Jade and Connor have spent all their lives here. They have family here, people they can depend on, but I'm wondering if anyone ever takes care of them. People can make sure they don't need anything or are available in case of an emergency, but does anyone do things for them because they care?

"There are plenty of people around to take care of you and your dad, Jade."

"I don't think that's what she means, Mom," Love whispers, bumping her shoulder against mine and motioning toward Jade.

I glance in her direction and notice her head bowed as she furiously wipes at her cheeks. I know that look. I've seen it reflecting at me in the mirror for years. Jade is more than likely carrying the weight of the world on her shoulders. Wanting to make things as easy for her dad as possible. Not to be too much trouble or cause him any stress, but deep down, all she wants is to be coddled occasionally.

"Sometimes I wish my mom was still around."

"Your mom is always here with you, Jade, even though you can't see her," I respond, wiping my hands on my pants. "I never had the honor of meeting your mother, but I know she and your dad love you very much."

"Listen to my mom. She knows things."

"I know you mean well, Audrey, but you couldn't possibly understand what it's like to grow up without a mom."

"Maybe not, but I know what it's like to lose one." I sigh, turning around and leaning against the counter beside Jade. "My mom died in a car accident a few months before Love's first birthday."

"Audrey, I'm so sorry."

"No need to be sorry. You couldn't have known." I

run my hand down her arm before giving her hand a light squeeze. "My mom was my best friend. I didn't have many of those growing up, and when she died, I was lost. I was completely alone in the world."

"Hey. What am I, chopped liver?" Love gasps in mock horror, clutching her chest for effect.

"Of course not, baby." I roll my eyes at Love's antics. "But my mom sent Bristol, then Leia and Selina, to help me through. And now those three are my family. I know they'd go to hell and back for Love and me. No questions asked."

"Moral of the story is that you have my mom and me now, Jade. We'll always be here for you and your dad. If you need anything, anything at all, you only need to call, and we'll come running."

"So, if I say I want homemade pancakes and sausage for breakfast tomorrow, you'll come by and make them?" Jade looks over at me hopefully.

"I'll ask you what time you'd like me to be here."

"Mom makes the best pancakes." Love smiles, throwing her arm over Jade's shoulder and pulling her to her side. "We're like a fungus. You're never getting rid of us."

"Good, because I don't want either of you to ever leave." Jade smiles before swatting Love on the butt. "Now, back to work."

Love and I give her a mock salute before returning to our duties and getting started.

I meant every word I said to Jade about my friends.

I'd never have made it through everything, after what happened to my parents, without Bristol. She's been my rock through the tough times, as well as Leia and Selina. I may not have known them as long, but they are two of the best friends I could ever ask for. These three are my family; our bond is stronger than blood. We are the family that chose each other, and I hope Jade and Love will form a similar bond, as well.

"My dad really likes you, Audrey. Do you like him, even a little?" She asks in a small voice.

My head whips to the side, Jade's emerald-green eyes pleading with me to answer in the affirmative. Not wanting to get her hopes up, I answer carefully. "Of course, I like your dad. Would I be going through all this trouble to make sure he rests if I didn't?"

Love rolls her eyes at me as she leans forward. "You know exactly what she meant, Mom. We both see the way the two of you look at each other."

"Not to mention we caught you kissing the other night."

"Wait, you saw us?" I gasp in shock.

"Duh. Why else do you think we've been doing everything we can to push you together?"

"Oh, you two." I wag my finger at them both. "But Love knows I've sworn off men after the last fiasco we went through."

"Connor is nothing like Ian, and you know it!" Love raises her voice slightly before apologizing quietly. "I know you're scared, Mom, but Jade and I want the both of you to be happy."

"My dad has always said I'm everything he needs in life, but he needs someone out there who can love him romantically." Jade hangs her head as Love pulls her in for a one-armed hug.

"Jade, your dad is an amazing man. I'm sure someone equally as amazing will love both of you to the end of time." I give her a sad smile before turning back to the dishes.

"But that person can be you, Audrey," Jade replies hopefully, followed quickly by Love.

"Just think about it, Mom. I know you said you wanted to focus on making a life here for us before getting into a relationship, but men like Connor don't come along every day. You don't want to miss your chance because you were afraid of getting hurt."

Not bothering to look up at either girl, I say, "Enough with the love advice. I know your name is Love, but the day I take relationship advice from my fourteen-year-old daughter will be the end of my dating life."

Both girls giggle as we finish up the dishes in silence. As soon as the last dish is put away in the kitchen, the three of us head to the living room and find Connor fast asleep on the couch. Jade heads toward him and pulls a blanket off the back of the couch, covering him up. "He's down for the count. I gave him one of those muscle relaxers before Love and I came to help you with the dishes."

Love shakes her head from beside me. "We told him to go upstairs and lie down, but he's so stubborn."

"That's my dad. He's always so strong, even when he needs to listen to someone else." Jade leans down and gives her dad a gentle kiss on the forehead before addressing us again. "Thanks so much for making him go to the hospital, and for making us dinner."

I raise my hands in defense. "It was no trouble at all. It was my fault he fell."

Love and Jade both have a laugh at my expense before I chime in, "Okay, ladies. Love and I need to head home, but text us if you or your dad need anything. We'll be back in the morning for breakfast. I have to teach a class tomorrow, but Love can stay here and help."

"I think I can manage him by myself, Audrey," Jade rebuts, but I'll hear none of that.

"I insist. Besides, didn't you say you wanted homemade pancakes for breakfast?"

"Okay, you twisted my arm. I'll text Love when we are awake and moving in the morning."

Love and I both give Jade a hug as we head for the door, but I stop to have one last look at Connor. I want nothing more than to curl up with him on the couch and never move, but I need to make sure the girls both understand we are nothing but friends.

"Night, honey. Make sure you lock up when we leave," I tell Jade as she slowly closes the door. I wait until I hear the deadbolt lock before Love and I turn and head toward home.

After spending the evening with Connor and Jade, I realize that's the one thing Love and I have been missing all these years—a family. People to come home to who love and care for us as much as we care for them. Here's to hoping that my attraction to Connor does not ruin this for either of us.

eleven

audrey

"Here goes nothing," I whisper to myself as I shuffle the deck of tarot cards a few times before placing the stack flat on the table and cutting it.

I haven't felt the need to use my tarot cards since we first moved here a little over a month ago, but right now, I'm in desperate need of some guidance.

"How will having a relationship with Connor Bennet effect Love and me? I whisper into the kitchen before taking a deep breath and flipping over a card. I gasp in surprise as I look down at the Two of Cups. "Huh, that's not what I was expecting."

This seems like the first time in years that the cards have given me the answer that I wanted. There is no hidden meaning or secret subtext to getting the Two of Cups when asking a relationship question. This card signifies the union of two souls. Although, it's not only used to describe romantic relationships but also good friendships and partnerships between two people based on a mutual understanding. That describes Connor and me in spades. We're both single parents, have a secret love for Disney movies, and prefer spending time with our children over just about anything else.

"See? Even the deck is telling you to give Connor a chance," Love chimes in from behind me. "Can you stop avoiding him now?"

It's been a few weeks since Connor injured his back, and things have finally gone relatively back to normal. I've gotten into a routine at work and even managed to get most of the house unpacked, which was a huge undertaking. Jade and Love have dance classes every Tuesday and Thursday night, and if they aren't in class together, they text each other back and forth until the wee hours of the morning.

"I haven't been avoiding Connor. I've just been busy with work and unpacking."

I'm only in partial denial. Bristol has been keeping me busy at the studio. I'm working at the studio four times a week and the odd class on the weekends, ensuring that my schedule remains flexible in case Love needs anything or an emergency arises. But my schedule isn't nearly as full as I'd like.

"Whatever you say, Mom. If it wasn't for the texts he sends you almost every day, I doubt you'd have spoken to him since the doctor gave him a clean bill of health weeks ago."

After spending time taking care of Connor, I know deep down he's nothing like Ian. Not only is he drop-dead gorgeous, but he's an amazing father and friend.

He's completely devoted to Jade, but he seems to have developed a soft spot for Love, as well. He always goes out of his way to check on her after dance class and makes a point to bring her favorite treat from Just the Drip whenever he picks up Jade from class. I expected him to have started to ignore Love, but he's done the exact opposite. I know deep down that even if I never speak to him again, if Love needs anything, he'll be there with bells on.

"It wasn't weeks ago," I mumble, knowing Love is right. "And we don't text all the time."

"Okay, maybe you don't talk while you're working, but I know for a fact that Auntie Bristol, Auntie Selina, and Auntie Leia aren't texting you all night long. They have lives."

"Rude. Besides, how do you know that?" I scoff, knowing damn well these four have been up to something.

Earlier this week, Leia, Selina, and Bristol all started wanting to know more about what was going on with Connor and me. Wanting to know how things went during dinner at his house and, more importantly, when I was going to let Connor take me on a date—the one thing I've been desperately trying to avoid. I know if I go on a date with Connor, that will lead to something more, which will lead to a relationship, which could blow up in my face. It is one of the main reasons I pulled out my tarot cards today. I want to go on a date with Connor, but all those pesky what-if questions keep swirling around in my mind. Love is doing amazing here in Tyson's Creek, not to mention this is the first place that's felt like home since my parents died. How can I risk ruining all of this for a man that I've only known for a month?

"Because we have a group chat. Those three are about to take matters into their own hands and force you to talk to Connor."

"They wouldn't dare."

"You know as well as I do they would." She narrows her eyes at me as her phone chimes loudly, signaling an incoming text. I don't even have to ask who it is. Love's eyes scan the screen before she turns her attention back to me. "Jade wants to know when we're going to come over again for dinner," Love questions as she plops down into a seat near the breakfast nook.

"I don't know. I need to check my schedule with Bristol."

"Nurture Space closes at six p.m., Mom."

"And? I came here to help your Auntie Bristol with anything she needs, and sometimes that means staying late at work."

"You're avoiding them, aren't you?"

"No. What makes you say that?" My voice raises slightly, knowing full well that Love is right.

When Connor was recovering from his fall, we spent almost every day, before and after work, at their place. Love and I headed over to Connor's house to make breakfast and check on him. We'd have a loud breakfast full of laughter before I had to head to work. Love stayed at their house to make sure Connor was resting, and the two of them would report his behavior, good or bad, to me when I let them know I was on my way to make dinner or grab them to head off to dance class. Afterward, we would have a nice dinner together, then settle in around the television for a movie before Love and I headed home for the night.

On the nights the girls convinced me to let Love spend the night, Connor and I would have deep conversations. We talked about my lack of relationship with Love's father and how hard it was taking care of her all on my own. I even told him about all my different careers and my tendency to let fate make choices for the two of us most of the time. Unlike most men, he never made me feel like a lunatic or that I wasn't doing what was best for my daughter.

He listened to all my stories and even talked about his late wife, Lydia. Anyone with eyes could tell that she still holds a piece of his heart; he even still wears his wedding ring. My concern is that he doesn't have room in his heart for anyone else.

"Hmm, the fact that we haven't been to Jade's for almost three weeks. Or that every time I mention going over to their house to hang out, you change the subject. Or—"

"I get it, Love." I sigh, pinching the bridge of my nose between my thumb and index fingers. "We need to head out before I'm late for work. You can hang out with your

Auntie Bristol and me or Auntie Selina and Emersyn before class."

"Okay, Mom. But you can't avoid them forever." She huffs before stomping toward the front door.

"Teenagers are even worse than toddlers," I mumble to myself before grabbing my keys off the hook and heading out the door.

Love doesn't say another word as we drive downtown, leaving me alone with my thoughts on what to do with whatever this is between Connor and me. I need to put on my big girl panties and make a decision, but hell if I know what that is. On the one hand, I can see the life I could have with Connor, the family I've always dreamed of, but on the other hand, I could end up right where I was when I arrived here—heartbroken and completely lost.

I sigh loudly as I pull into a parking spot near the dance studio, no closer to making a decision than I was when I left the house.

"Bye, Mom. I'm going to go hang out with Auntie Selina." Love gives me a quick kiss on the cheek and climbs out of the car.

My head drops back onto the seat as I whisper into the empty car, "I'm here to make a life for me and Love, not fall for mister tall, dark, and handsome."

But you want him, don't you?

"Shut up, you," I respond to the nagging voice in the back of my mind, reminding me that if it was any other time, Connor would be exactly what I'm looking for.

"I'm not falling in love with Connor Bennett!" I shout inside my car before shutting it off, hopping out, and slamming the door behind me for good measure.

"It doesn't really work like that, hun." I spin around, plastering myself to the driver's side door as I come face to face with Bristol.

"When did you become a ninja? You appeared out of nowhere," I reply, placing two fingers on my neck to check my pulse.

"Stop being so dramatic, Audrey. I've been standing here for a while. Love even gave me a kiss and a hug before running into the dance studio, but you were too into the conversation with yourself to notice."

"Whatever." I roll my eyes for good measure before squeezing between her belly and the car next to me. "Shouldn't you be teaching a class or something?"

"I should be, but we finished early. I saw you pull in and figured I'd come and say hi."

"Okay. Hi. Now, if you'll excuse me, I need to get to work," I mumble, trying to avoid any further conversation about Connor and me, but before I can head toward the studio, Bristol places a gentle hand on my shoulder.

"Dang it," Bristol says in mock horror. "I completely forgot to tell you that your class this evening was canceled."

"Why?"

"Because I own the place and have barely spent any time with my best friend since she moved to town a few weeks ago because she's been hiding," she deadpans, placing both her hands on my hips.

Connor isn't the only person I've been keeping at arm's length over the last few weeks. I haven't been avoiding my friends, per se, but I don't know how to answer all their questions about what's going on between us.

"I haven't been hiding. I've been busy trying to get us settled and Love ready to start school in a few months."

"Love is fine, and I doubt it's taken you this long to unpack. You don't want to talk about what's going on between you and Connor Bennett."

"There's nothing going on, Bristol."

"Audrey Wilde, why do you always have to be so stubborn?" She sighs loudly. "If the two of you are meant to be, there really isn't anything you can do about it."

"Just like you and Seth?"

"We aren't talking about me and the father of my child," Bristol threads her arm through mine and pulling me toward the dance studio.

"You and I both know that you are in love with Seth. It shouldn't matter that he's in the military, but for some reason, you can't bring yourself to let him know how you feel."

"I refuse to let my baby grow up feeling like they're second in anyone's heart." Bristol huffs as we stroll toward the dance studio.

"Is there a reason we aren't heading into Nurture Space?"

"I'm not the only person you've been avoiding. Since your class was canceled, I figured we could hang out with Selina for a little while and catch up."

"Sure. You just want backup to give me the third degree," I respond, barely above a whisper to ensure no one overhears what we're saying. "But don't change the subject. Seth isn't your dad. Just like you continue to tell me Connor isn't Ian."

No one in town knows who the father of Bristol's baby is. At first, she wanted to keep it a secret to ensure she was the one to tell him, but when she never received any contact from him, she decided to never speak of it again. I only found out by accident. Bristol called me completely heartbroken and terrified of raising a baby on her own, something I know a lot about. After calming her down, I let her know that she wasn't alone and that we'd all be there for her and the baby after it was born. She told her parents it was a silly one-night stand. They were disappointed, but they never pushed for more information besides that.

"I know Seth isn't my father, but he's a Marine. The Marine Corps is his life, and it will be until the day he retires, no matter what he says. It just makes things between the two of us even more complicated. The Corps always came first in my father's eyes. Birthdays, graduations, wedding anniversaries were all forgotten if the Corp needed him." Bristol's hand absentmindedly rubbing her baby bump as she pulls open the door. "He didn't even put up a fight when we had to move from

Louisiana, leaving you and Love all alone. I refuse for my baby to feel the same way…" Bristol trails off as she pulls open the door.

Thankfully, there's no one else in the waiting room. I wouldn't put it past Bristol to be hiding Connor in the waiting room so he could blindside me and ask me on a date.

"The man practically laid his heart on the line for you that night, Bristol. What else do you want from him?" I sigh, dropping my bag onto one of the chairs in the waiting room.

"A phone call or a letter would be nice. I haven't heard a peep from him since he deployed. If he wanted anything to do with me, he would have called."

"You know how hard it is to call people from overseas."

"He'd find a way if he really wanted to," Bristol grumbles as she pulls out a chair and takes a seat. We stare at each other for a few minutes before she smiles brightly and changes the subject. "A little birdy told me that Connor is looking for the perfect opportunity to ask you on a date."

"Is that so?"

"Don't be like that, Audrey. Connor likes you. You should be nice and put the man out of his misery. You've been avoiding him, and we all know it."

"I've been busy, not avoiding him," I mutter, knowing that I'm full of crap. I promised Connor he could make me dinner one night when he was feeling better, but I expected I could use the girls as a buffer. However, the last night we all had dinner together, he made it perfectly clear he wanted an adults-only evening, and I've been ducking his attempts to ask me out ever since. I'm sure he plans on making a big deal out of it, thinking that my fear of embarrassment will stop me from turning him down.

"You can't avoid him anymore," Bristol says as her phone chimes softly. "Because I may have let him know you'd be here today."

"What happened to chicks before dicks?" I growl, grabbing my bag and contemplating making a hasty retreat out the back door.

"This is the same thing. Friends don't let friends do dumb shit. It's just a date, Audrey. What's the worst that could happen?"

"You are so lucky I love you..."

"And you're lucky I love you. That's why when Connor asks, you're going to tell him you'd be happy to go to dinner with him." Just as I'm about to reply, the tiny bell above the door sounds, and Bristol shoves me toward it.

"Just the woman I've been looking for." Connor's deep voice causes me to freeze in place.

Well, here goes nothing.

twelve

connor

"Fancy meeting you here." Audrey's voice quivers. I have it on the best authority that she's been avoiding me for the last few weeks, but that ends now.

"Did you forget our deal?" I smirk, stepping closer toward her.

"I didn't forget. I've just been busy. When would you like for us to come over for dinner?"

"Oh..." I rub the back of my neck, my entire face flushing with embarrassment. My palms sweat as my heart pounds inside my chest.

Audrey has been avoiding seeing me for weeks. We still chat on the phone almost nightly, but every time I bring up our date, she changes the subject immediately. I know she fears being hurt, but I thought all the time we spent together while I was recovering from my fall had changed her mind. I called Bristol, hoping for some advice, but she told me to come to the Barre Studio tonight, ready to ask Audrey out on a date, before promptly hanging up on me.

I told Vance what happened, and he insisted on tagging along with me to drop off Jade at dance class. I have a feeling they are all waiting in the wings for the fireworks to begin. Cornering Audrey like this seems like a bad move, but I need to know where I stand. I have a feeling that if it was up to her, she'd continue avoiding me until I gave up. Too bad for her, I have no intention of doing so. I want to explore this connection between Audrey and me, and I have no intention of giving up until I do so.

"I was hoping we'd be able to have dinner alone, giving us a chance to get to know each other. I love my daughter, but I don't make a habit of taking her on dates."

"This isn't a date, Connor." Audrey sighs before stepping to the side and heading toward the door. "I promised you dinner, not a date."

"Is there something wrong with dating me?" I question as Vance comes strolling into the waiting room, making a beeline for Selina. I sigh loudly, not wanting to deal with whatever is about to happen between those two. Selina has been desperately trying to get Vance to leave her alone, but my best friend is insistent, just like me. I keep trying to tell Selina to just go on a date with him, and then he'll leave her alone, but she won't listen, only solidifying my position that she's still in love with him.

I tug on Audrey's arm lightly, pulling her to a stop. "Hold on a moment. I want to watch Vance crash and burn with Selina." Audrey raises her eyebrow as I motion toward Vance and Selina standing near the door and creep forward. I place a finger over my mouth to signal her to stay quiet. As we move closer, I pick up their conversation.

"For the last time, Vance. There's no chance I'll ever go on a date with you." Selina crosses her arms over her chest and cocks her hip to the side.

"We used to be good together, Selina. What happened to the girl who loved me with all her heart?"

"She grew up." Selina huffs before spinning on her heels and heading into the back room.

I chuckle as I wrap my arm around Vance's shoulder. "How many times now has she turned you down?"

"I lost count, but I'm wearing her down. I can feel it." Vance flashes me a smile before focusing on Audrey. "Did he finally convince you to go on a date with him?"

She dips her head slightly before answering. "Not exactly."

I grimace. "It's not a date, man, just a quiet night with the girls."

"But you said..." I shove Vance in the shoulder before chiming in.

"I know what I said, but we're going to have dinner together as a family." I look directly into her eyes, attempting to convey how serious I am about the four of us becoming a family in the future.

"Sure, dinner with the girls sounds nice. When did

you want to get together?" Her cheeks flush a beautiful shade of light pink as she flashes me a shy smile.

I know I wanted a date with just the two of us, but for some reason, she's hesitant to be alone with me. I'd like to believe it's because she is falling for me, but I don't want to get my hopes up. At this point, I just want to spend more time with her. Although we've been sharing nightly text messages and phone calls, I want to be close to her. I want to see her smile at my jokes or watch as her eyes light up when she finds something funny. And the only way to do that is by proposing a family dinner because that's exactly what the four of us are.

We have been circling around each other ever since I got hurt. After spending so much time together, it's impossible for Jade and me to go back to the way things were. Our house has felt empty the last few weeks without Audrey and Love stopping by to check in and see how we are doing or to have dinner with the two of us. There is no way Audrey is going to go for being alone with me, so I chose the next best thing—family dinner.

"How about tonight? He doesn't have to be at work until the afternoon tomorrow, just in case you guys stay up chatting." Vance flashes us both a bright smile before slapping me on the back. "I'll be in the truck, waiting for you two."

Audrey covers her laugh with a cough. "Is he always like that?"

"Unfortunately, yes. But I couldn't ask for a better

friend. He has been there for Jade and me since she was born."

"It's great to have people around when you need them."

I run my hand down her arm, threading my fingers through hers and giving them a small squeeze. "Jade and I are here for both of you. We're family now."

Audrey's cheeks turn rosy pink as the girls come crashing out of the studio. Jade speaks first. "Can Love and I have a sleepover?"

Audrey nods her head as I squeeze her hand. "Sure thing. We're having dinner together tonight anyway." I flash her a bright smile. "Jade and I will head home to shower and get the grill started. We'll see you both in about an hour."

"Sounds good. I'm sure my mom wants to make a dessert or something to bring over. My mom says that my grandma always said to never visit someone empty-handed."

"Your grandma was a smart lady." I smile at her before wrapping my arm around her shoulder and giving her a hug. "So is your mom."

"She already said she'd go on a date with you, Connor." Love giggles as she tries to wiggle from my embrace.

"Not a date. A family dinner," I reply, planting a kiss on the top of her head before taking a step back.

"Family dinner, huh?" Love smiles brightly at me before reaching for her mom's other hand and pulling her toward the door. "Jade, I'll text you when we are on our way over." She waves over her head before heading out the door with Audrey in tow.

"You two are up to something. Aren't you, Squirt?" I wrap my arm around Jade's shoulder, pulling her tightly to my side and leading us toward the exit.

"No, never." Her voice raises slightly before she clears her throat. "Love and I just want to spend time together again. Is that too much to ask?"

I give her a kiss on the forehead as I push the door open. "It's nice having someone else in the house besides the two of us, isn't it?"

"I wouldn't mind if we made it a little more permanent, either." Jade pulls away and heads toward the truck, quickly spotting Vance sitting in the passenger seat. "Uncle Vance! Tell Dad to make a move on Audrey before she runs away."

Vance throws his hands up in surrender as she opens the half door and slides in. "I've been telling him, but he's taking his sweet time with it. Strike while the iron is hot, I say."

"Have you gotten Selina to go out with you yet?" Jade asks before popping an ear bud into one ear. When Vance doesn't say anything, she continues. "That's what I thought."

"Shut it, Squirt. I'm wearing her down," Vance turns his attention toward me. "You're welcome, by the way. If I wouldn't have given you the idea of having dinner together tonight, you'd have been trying for another week to catch her off guard."

I send up a silent prayer of thanks for Vance's meddling ways. "Don't I know it, but this isn't a date. It's just the four of us having dinner together."

"That's not how you wanted it to be, is it?" Jade questions, cocking her head to the side.

"Not at all, but it's what makes her comfortable," I respond, eyeing her skeptically.

There's no doubt that Jade and Love know exactly how I feel about Audrey. Those two are thick as thieves, but who knows how they really feel about their parents being together? I know I've asked Jade about it, and she seems okay, but now that it's really happening, I want to check back in with her just to make sure. All it would take is one word from her to stop, and I would. No matter how my feelings for Audrey have grown over the last month, if Jade isn't happy, it's not happening.

"You really like her, don't you?"

"I do," I reply, not wanting to sugarcoat my feelings for Audrey. "Are you okay with that?"

"Dad, I'm fourteen, not two." Jade snorts before grabbing my hand and giving it a squeeze. "You deserve to be happy just like everyone else."

"I'm happy," I grumble, causing Vance to chuckle.

"Whatever you say, Dad." Jade shakes her head before releasing my hands and leaning back. "Love and I can hang out in my room after dinner and give you two time to chat. That will be the perfect time for you to make your move."

I peek at Jade in the rearview mirror as I back out of the spot and head home. "I don't want to discuss my moves with you."

"I don't want you to, either. I'm speaking hypothetically." Vance lets out a boisterous laugh, slapping his knee a few times before gripping his stomach.

I shake my head at his antics. "I can't wait for you to have a teenage daughter."

"Neither can I. Selina and I will have gorgeous children."

"Wishful thinking," I mutter to myself before focusing my attention back on the road.

Jade is right. I need to use this opportunity to get closer to Audrey. I know someone hurt her badly in the past. It's understandable she has trust issues when it comes to men. I hadn't thought about having a relationship in years, believing there was no one else in this world for me but Lydia. That is, until I met Audrey. Just being near her completes me in a way I didn't know was possible. Now the only thing I need to do is convince her to take a chance on me. Not a hard task, not at all.

thirteen

audrey

"Hold on a second, Love." I pull my hand from her grasp. "You have dance class in a few minutes. What's gotten into you?" I stop dead in my tracks and cross my arms.

"I told Auntie Selina that I was missing class today." Love turns toward me and mirrors my position. "I'm not letting you get out of having dinner with Connor."

"Who said anything about trying to get out of it? He asked, and I said we would come over for dinner." I step around her and hit the button to unlock the car.

"Mom, I heard you two talking. He didn't want to have dinner with all of us. He wanted to take you on a date." Love pulls her door open and drops into the seat.

I open my door and take a seat. Before I have a chance to start the engine, Love sighs. "I just want you to be happy, Mom. What are you so afraid of?" Love stares into my eyes, searching for an answer.

I have plenty of things to be afraid of, but nothing more than whatever this is between Connor and me. Who knew that after a few stolen kisses and a heavy make out session, that the connection I feel with him would be off the charts. It's as if our souls are in perfect tune with each other, and it freaks me out. Have I ever felt like this before? No. Do I anticipate ever feeling like this again? Also no. But that doesn't make me any less terrified about crossing the line in the sand.

I promised myself and Love that I'd put her first, that I'd grow up and stop searching for someone to love me and focus on what's best for her. Being here in Tyson's Creek is what's best for Love. She's thriving here. Everyone here has practically adopted the two of us as their own, and I don't want to jeopardize that if whatever this is between Connor and me blows up in my face.

"I'm not afraid of anything. I promised you that I was going to remain focused on getting settled in and making a home for the two of us here." I quickly start the engine and reverse out of the parking spot, pointing the car towards home.

"You can fall in love and make a home for us at the same time. It doesn't have to be one or the other." Love ends the conversation by shoving her ear buds into her ears.

Love isn't wrong, but is it worth the risk? I refuse to let history repeat itself. Every time I open myself up to love, it blows up in my face. With Trey, I was enthralled with the popular boy who gave me attention. He treated me differently than anyone else and made me feel special before taking what he wanted from me and disappearing. The only good thing that came from that relationship was Love, and I could never regret her, but I didn't learn from my mistakes.

I became more careful about my relationships after Love was born, wanting to protect her as much as I could from any of my relationships. Ian was the only one of my significant others that Love met, but even that blew up in my face. Now, there is Connor and Jade. Jade has become such an intricate part of Love's life that I refuse to take the chance that she might lose that.

If things between Connor and me don't work out, there is so much more at stake than a broken heart. It will destroy me and any chance I have of creating a life for Love and me here.

Tyson's Creek is a small town; everyone knows everyone here. The last thing I want is for everyone to know how Connor broke my heart. I won't be able to handle the sad looks every time I'm out in public. It's better to stop things before they get started, protecting my heart and Love from having to leave the first place we've been able to call home since she was a little girl.

"He isn't wearing his ring anymore," Love mumbles, her attention still focused out the window.

"What?" My head snaps in her direction.

"Jade told me her dad took his wedding ring off a few weeks ago."

"Why in the world would he do that?" My grip on the steering wheel tightens.

"Because he likes you, Mom, and he isn't afraid to let everyone know that." Love pulls her ear buds out of her ears. "Sometimes you need to take a chance on love to find what you've always been looking for. You can't spend the rest of your life being afraid of what might happen."

"You believe Connor is the one for me?" I whisper as I turn into our driveway and shut the car off.

"He may be, but you'll never know until you give it a shot."

"Are you sure this isn't because Jade is your new BFF, and you have always wanted a sibling?"

Love giggles, breaking the tension in the air. "Jade is a bonus. I mean, I used to ask for a baby brother for my birthday and Christmas when I was younger."

I let out a full belly laugh. "You did! You were so disappointed when you came downstairs Christmas morning and only found your favorite toys under the tree."

"I stopped asking when I discovered where babies came from. The thought of you doing *that* with anyone is disgusting. I'll settle for a sister I already love. You and Connor can get to work on the brother after you get together."

"We haven't even gone on a date yet, and you're already planning for a baby brother?"

"What can I say? Jade and I have a good feeling about you two. All you need to do is open your heart to the possibility of love. The universe will do the rest."

"The universe, huh? I thought you didn't believe in fate and all that nonsense."

"I don't, but you do, and I respect that. Besides, you

asked the cards for advice this morning, and they told you that things between you and Connor will work out. All you need to do now is listen to them."

"Easier said than done," I mutter to myself as we both hop out of the car and head for the front door. "Whether Connor and I are together or not, you and Jade will still be close. You know that, right?"

"Of course, Jade and I will." Love grabs both of my hands. "But I know relationships are complicated and messy. I also know that things might not work out between you and Connor, but Jade and I have a good feeling about it."

"You two have been talking about us?" I smirk as I pull her into my chest for a hug.

"We're teenagers. Talking about everyone's love life is in our DNA," she mumbles into my shoulder before giving me a tight squeeze. "Everyone knows how much you two like each other; it's written all over your faces. The only thing we ask is that you give him a chance. Please? For me?"

I pull back and stare into my daughter's eyes. "I make no promises."

Love throws a fist into the air. "At least you didn't say no. I call this progress."

"Come on. I need to figure out what to make for dessert." I put my key into the lock and turn the key. Love pushes past me, heading directly up the stairs.

"Make something out of a box! You need to have

enough time to get ready," she shouts from the top of the stairs.

I look down at my simple white shirt with black yoga pants. "What's wrong with what I'm wearing?"

"Everything!" she shouts before the sound of the door shutting filters down the stairs.

I check the time, drop my things on the table, and head directly toward the pantry. I won't have enough time to make something fancy, but I notice the ingredients to make a batch of caramel brownies. Pulling out all the ingredients, I grab everything else I need from around the kitchen and get to baking.

As soon as I place the pan of brownies into the oven, Love comes barreling into the kitchen. "Now it's time to get ready! Go take a shower and wash your hair. I picked out a few outfits for you to choose from on your bed."

"I need to set the timer to make sure the brownies don't burn." I look down at myself, noticing a few smudges of caramel and chocolate on my shirt and arms. I really do need to shower. I quickly set the timer and make my way out of the kitchen.

When I enter my bedroom, I head directly for my bed and notice the outfits Love chose for me. Only one catches my eye, a form-fitting pair of jeans and a black scoop-neck top.

"Don't you think these outfits are a little too much for dinner as friends?" I question as Love comes rushing into my room behind me, flopping down on the bed.

"Nope. Face it, Mom. You're hot. If you are really going to figure out how Connor feels about you, then the first step is discovering if he's physically attracted to you."

"I really don't want to be having this conversation with you right now," I grumble, pinching the bridge of my nose as I look between the three outfits.

The bright red wrap dress she has laid out on the bed beside the jeans seems to be a little much for a quiet dinner at home with the girls. If this is really a date, I need to look casual. The other outfit is hideous and off the list of possibilities. The jeans and top are just sexy enough to get Connor's blood pumping but not look like I'm trying too hard.

"I could always call Auntie Bristol, Selina, and Leia to come help you choose," Love replies, giving me a knowing look.

"No, thank you. So physical attraction is important for sure, but this is just a dinner between friends. Nothing more."

"Whatever you need to tell yourself, Mom. Either way, I'm not letting you out of the house without choosing one of these outfits."

"Fine. I'll worry about it when I get out of the shower," I say under my breath before heading to the bathroom.

I shower quickly, not forgetting to wash my hair, then head to my dresser to grab a bra and panties. I pull out the drawer, but before I can grab anything, it slams shut.

"You almost took my fingers off, Love," I growl before grabbing the bra and panties dangling from her finger.

"You'd have put on granny panties and the ugliest bra you own." Love shoves a pair of sexy black panties and a matching bra in my direction. "You need to have the right ones to compliment your outfit."

"How do you know what outfit I chose?" I snatch the panties from her hand, drop my towel, and step into them before shoving my arms through the straps of my bra.

"Because I chose two outfits you would hate to guarantee you chose the right one." Love gives me a sly smile before grabbing the jeans and shirt off the bed and shoving them into my arms. I take a moment to look at Love. She's changed into a similar outfit to the one she chose for me, but her shirt says, *If you think I'm hot, you should see my mother.*

"Trying to prove a point?" I motion toward her shirt before stepping into my jeans and pulling them over my hips.

"It's true, isn't it?" She gives me her best set of puppy dog eyes before we both cackle with laughter. "Hurry and finish getting dressed."

"Who is the parent in this relationship?" I mutter as I pull my top over my head.

"You are, but if I left things up to you, there's no telling what you would have worn."

"Yes, ma'am." I give my bossy daughter a mock salute before following her into the bathroom.

"Now for your hair." Love pushes me down onto the toilet as she bends down to pull hair products out from under the sink.

"We are going to go with curly and simple," she says, holding up my diffuser and curl cream.

I nod my head in approval, and Love drops a large drop of curl cream into her hands before passing me the bottle. We both take turns running the cream through my hair before I flip my head over and begin twisting sections into curls. Once all the sections are finished, I flip my head back over, and Love plugs in the diffuser.

"The natural look for makeup," Love shouts over the noise of the dryer before dropping my makeup bag in my lap.

"Was there another option?" I roll my eyes at her in my compact mirror before I begin applying my makeup.

Love cuts off the hair dryer before pronouncing me ready to leave. "The brownies!" I shout in panic.

"No worries. I grabbed them out of the oven and cut them before I came upstairs."

I sigh in relief. "Did you put them on the nice platter we got from Bristol last Christmas?"

"This isn't my first rodeo." Love rolls her eyes as she chooses jewelry for me to wear and nudges me toward the mirror.

As I put it on, doubt creeps into my mind. "What am I doing? There is no way this can be anything more than friendship between Connor and me."

"Just give him a chance, Mom," Love whispers as she

places my deck of tarot cards into my hand. "Ask the cards again if it makes you feel better, but we both already know what they're going to say. Connor is perfect for you. For us, but none of that can happen unless you give him a chance to prove it."

I look down at the box of cards and wonder if my daughter is right. I've always used the cards to help me make important decisions in my life, but my ability to interpret what they were saying was shaken after my relationship with Ian. I shuffle the deck of cards in my hands, trying to think of the exact question to ask that will set my nerves at ease but come up empty.

I've been so focused on all the bad things that have happened in my life that maybe this time, instead of focusing on what could go wrong, I should try and focus on what could go right. Things with Connor and me might crash and burn, but what if they don't? What if he really is the man that I've been looking for my entire life, and I miss my opportunity to find out?

"You know what? I'm good," I say with conviction before placing the deck of cards on the top of my dresser and turning toward Love.

"I'm proud of you, Mom." Love wraps her arms around my waist and gives me a quick squeeze.

"You know what? I'm proud of myself, too."

"Hurry or we will be late," Love calls, pulling me toward the stairs.

"It's now or never," I whisper to myself. I don't need

a deck of cards to tell me Connor and I are attracted to each other; I know that deep down in my soul. Maybe, just maybe, this time, my heart and the cards are in agreement.

fourteen

connor

I pull the steaks and asparagus off the grill and head back inside. As I enter the kitchen, Jade comes barreling down the stairs. "Do you need help with anything?"

"I think I have everything covered, Squirt."

"Can you please—you know what? Never mind. You're going to call me Squirt no matter what. I might as well embrace it."

"That's the spirit." I chuckle, planting a kiss on her cheek before placing the plate of food into the oven.

"Dinner is ready. I grabbed beer, wine, and soda from the store earlier. Am I missing anything?" I mutter to myself as I go over the checklist in my head.

The moment Audrey said she'd have dinner with us tonight, I was beyond excited. Thankfully, I had almost everything I needed to make an amazing meal. After dropping Vance off at his truck, I made a quick stop at the store for beer and a good wine before heading home and getting started on dinner.

"Everything is going to be perfect." Jade wraps her

arms around my waist from behind. "But you might want to shower before she gets here."

"Yeah, that would be a good idea." I give her arm a squeeze before unwrapping them from around my waist. "There's no way I'm going to win Audrey over if I smell as if I've been at work all day."

I look down at myself. I have on a simple pair of jeans, a white T-shirt, and a button-up flannel shirt over the top. I rolled the sleeves up just above my elbows while I was grilling, but the last thing I want to do is look like a slob. I want this date to be perfect, or as perfect as it can be, with our two teenage daughters joining us.

"Can you set the table while I run upstairs and take a quick shower?"

"You got it." Jade gives me a mock salute before opening the cabinet and pulling out a stack of plates. "Everything is going to be okay, Dad. There's no need for you to be so nervous."

"Am I that obvious?" I chuckle, rubbing the back of my neck.

Everything seems to be riding on this dinner with Audrey and Love. This might be my only chance to prove to her that I'm not like the men she's dated in the past, and I'm in it for the long haul. If I ruin this date, it could also sink any chance of Audrey wanting to become more than friends.

"Only a smidge." Jade snickers. "I've never seen you go on a date or even look at another woman before Audrey moved here. She's special, isn't she?"

"She is." I wrap my arms around her, pulling her to my chest. "I feared letting someone into our lives before meeting Audrey. Your mom left a big set of shoes to fill."

"Is that why you took off your wedding ring?"

"Yes and no," I pull back slightly, gripping her chin between my fingers and forcing her to look at me. "I took it off because it was time."

"Time to move on and find love again?"

"Exactly." I wink at her before smiling brightly.

"Audrey is good for you. For both of us. You seem lighter and smile more, too."

"I *feel* lighter if I'm being honest. I used to believe that I'd never find someone who I felt as strongly about as your mother. Until recently, I believed she was the only woman I'd ever love—besides you, of course—but then I met Audrey, and suddenly, falling in love again didn't seem so impossible."

"Are you in love with Audrey?" Jade's eyes widen in surprise, her eyes swimming with hope as she stares back at me.

This is a question that I've been asking myself for weeks, wondering if it is possible to be in love with someone I've only known for a little over a month. I've yet to come up with a response. The connection between the two of us is soul-deep, as if we complete each other in a way that no one else could. However, it's not the same as the love I will always have for Lydia. I know deep down that Lydia was one of the greatest loves of my life. Until recently, if anyone asked me if I believed in having more than one true love in my life, I'd have laughed in their face. But now that I've met Audrey, I know we're meant to be together. The universe sent Audrey to us, not as a replacement for Lydia, but to fill the gaping hole in our lives that was created after Lydia passed.

"I may be, Squirt. Only time will tell." I plant a kiss on the top of her head as she squeals loudly.

"I knew it. I knew it." She jumps up and down in place, clapping her hands. "I always wanted to have a sister, but Love and I also want a brother."

"Hold on, Jade. Aren't you getting a little ahead of yourself?"

"Nope. I'm not saying we want one right now, but if you could have a baby before we graduate high school and go away to college, that would be appreciated."

"I barely convinced Audrey to go on a date. It only worked because I used you and Love as a buffer. It's going to be a long time before we even broach the subject of babies."

"Dad! Everything is going to be perfect. Just trust me!" She groans as she takes the stack of plates and heads toward the dining room. "I got things covered down here. Go upstairs and shower."

"Thanks, Squirt," I reply before turning on my heels and heading for the stairs.

"I got your back, Dad!" Jade shouts from the dining room.

I rush up the stairs and strip naked before jumping in the shower. As I lather up my body with soap, thoughts of Audrey fill my mind. I wonder if she's as nervous as I am and if she's been avoiding me for this very reason.

I haven't been shy about letting Audrey know how I feel about her, but something is holding her back from taking that next step with me, and I'm sure I know what it is. She told me she's been hurt in the past, but it has to go deeper than that. Love's dad has never been in the picture, so the idea she's still in love with him after almost fifteen years later isn't out of the question, but wouldn't she be upfront about that? It seems her ex may have hurt her deeper than I thought. Since she agreed to our sort-of date, I'm hoping she's ready to open up to me, even if it's only a little.

"I need to be patient. Take things slowly. If it's meant to be, it will be," I say, taking a deep breath before rinsing off and jumping out of the shower. Instead of drying off, I wrap a towel around my waist and head into my closet in search of some clothes.

I have no idea what I should wear on a date, especially one where my teenage daughter will also be present. I don't own anything fancy. I'm a jeans and flannel shirt kind of guy and wear the same things almost every day. But tonight is special.

I hear a soft knock on my bedroom door. "Need some help?" Jade's voice filters through the door.

"Help would be nice, but let me put on some pants first." I grab the first pair of boxers I find, pulling them on along with a pair of basic blue jeans before heading for my bedroom door.

I pull open the door and find Jade holding a hanger on the edge of her finger. A black T-shirt is hanging beneath a dark blue-and-gray button-up over the top of it.

"Where did you get that?"

"Uncle Vance. He just dropped it off. He figured you'd have a hard time finding something nice to wear."

I grab the hanger from her and head back into the closet, closing the door. I immediately pull off my jeans and replace them with a pair of dark-wash jeans, before pulling the black T-shirt over my head and sliding my arms into the button-up shirt. I roll the sleeves up to my elbows to ensure I don't get too warm while we have dinner and then grab a pair of socks. I debate for a few moments about shoes before deciding against them, and then I open the door and step out.

I find Jade seated on the edge of my bed, her phone stuck in front of her face and her fingers flying across the screen. "Should I shave?"

"No way. Chicks dig the scruffy mountain man look." Jade smiles before typing out one final text and shoving her cell phone into her back pocket.

"What if Audrey doesn't?"

"She does. Trust me." Jade pushes off the bed and heads toward the door. "Well, they should be here soon, and Uncle Vance is waiting downstairs."

"What are you up to, Squirt?"

"I'm giving you the quiet dinner with Audrey you

wanted. Uncle Vance is going to take Love and me to the movies, and then we're going to have a sleepover."

"A sleepover, huh? Did either of you ask Audrey before concocting this plan? She agreed to Love sleeping over here. Not your uncle's house."

"Asking Audrey wasn't my job, Dad. I came up with a plan. Love is on her own on how to ensure things with her mom go off without a hitch."

"Whatever you say." I chuckle, pulling her to my side for a hug. "Thanks for the backup, Squirt."

"No problem." She smiles before running down the stairs and directly into her uncle's arms.

"You clean up nice." Vance smiles as he plants a kiss on Jade's head.

"Thanks for the shirt and the alone time." I reach out my hand, and Vance grasps it tightly in his before pulling me in for a one-armed hug.

"Don't mention it. I have a feeling these two were going to find a way to get the two of you alone whether I helped or not."

"You're right." I attempt to turn toward the kitchen before Jade grabs my arm and pulls me toward the living room.

"Everything is fine. I set the table and grabbed one of the bottles of wine you bought and put it in the fridge." I give her a quizzical look before she clarifies, "Uncle Vance chose which wine you bought, and I put it in the fridge, but don't worry, it's all done."

"I wasn't worried until you mentioned your uncle

Vance." I sit down on the couch just as the doorbell rings, signaling their arrival.

"Now it's too late. Just relax. Uncle Vance, you head out to the truck, and I'll be right behind you."

"Thanks again for the help." I grip her by the arm as she tries to scurry by, pulling her into a hug.

"Always," she mumbles before hugging me back quickly and heading for the door.

Jade and Love are trying to help us spend time alone together, but I'm still unsure of where Audrey stands on the subject. I've known since the first moment I laid eyes on her that she'd be mine, but I need to figure out how to get her on the same page as me.

I hear footsteps coming my way as I push up off the couch and head in that direction, catching a glimpse of Audrey as she turns the corner and heads toward me. She has on a delicious pair of jeans that hug all her curves and a top that shows off just enough skin. Her gaze flicks to mine, as if I've called her name, and she pulls her lip between her teeth before dropping her head downward.

"Hey." Her breath hitches as our gazes meet again, and her caramel-colored eyes sparkle with the same need that burns like fire in my veins. "It seems our dinner with the girls isn't happening."

"Yeah. Vance asked if Jade could go to the movies with him and have a sleepover at his place. Did Love not tell you?" I chuckle softly as her eyes snap up to mine. A delicious shade of pink runs down her neck, disappearing into the top of her shirt and leaving me to wonder how far the color goes.

"She did, but not until we parked in your driveway. I have a feeling those two set us up."

"You'd be right," I breathe, my eyes wandering down her body as I stride toward her. Her eyes widen slightly as her hand tightens on the strap of her bag. I continue to inch closer; her eyes scan my body, as if committing it to memory before flicking back to my own.

"You look beautiful," I grunt, brushing my thumb across her bottom lip as I lean forward, my eyes focused on hers.

"Thank you," she whispers as I wrap my arm around her waist, pulling her against me.

We stare at each other for a few moments, waiting for the other to make the first move. I'm hanging on by a thread, the need to claim her lips almost overwhelming as she leans forward and brushes her lips against mine.

Electricity zips through my body as an unknown force pulls us closer together.

"You don't look too bad yourself," she mumbles against my mouth before nibbling on my bottom lip and running her tongue along it, begging for entrance.

"Thanks," I groan before threading my fingers into her hair and crushing our lips together.

Our lips mold together in sync, as if we've done this a million times. My tongue gently caresses the seam of her lips, begging for entrance as my free hand grips the back of her neck, eliciting a loud moan of pleasure from her. I plunge my tongue into her mouth, as if I'm trying to devour her whole. Fire burns in my veins as she slides her hands up my chest, wraps her arms around my neck, and pulls herself closer to my body.

"Audrey," I groan, nibbling on her lower lip. She leans her head back, giving me better access to her neck. I waste no time licking the curve of her throat, getting my first taste of her sweet skin. I grip her leg and pull it up slightly. She thrusts her warm center into my aching cock, causing both of us to groan in pleasure before lowering her leg back to the ground and taking a step back. Both of our chests heave as we come down from whatever happened a few moments ago. Her brown skin is flushed a beautiful shade of pink as my eyes zoom in on the red marks along her skin where I tasted her.

"I'd apologize, but I'm not sorry. I've spent more time than I'd like to admit dreaming about kissing you again."

Audrey ducks her head. "Thanks, I've never received a welcome like that before."

I step closer to her and place my finger under her chin, raising it slightly. "I'll make a habit of it."

She gives me a bright smile before responding, "I look forward to it."

I capture her lips with mine again before her belly rumbles, causing both of us to laugh. I lace our fingers together, placing a kiss on her hand. "Let's get you fed. The girls did a lot of scheming to give us time alone together. I don't want it to go to waste."

When we get closer to the table, I drop her hand and

pull her chair out for her. She gives me another shy smile before taking a seat. "Such a gentleman."

"You'd be surprised at the ungentlemanly thoughts I'm having about you at this moment." I give her a wink before taking the seat next to her. "Hope you like steak."

"I love it." She grabs a piece of steak and some asparagus off the platter. I do the same, noticing that Jade put together a salad and made mashed potatoes to go along with our dinner.

Audrey moans loudly. Her face is the picture of pure bliss as she licks her lips. "This is the best steak I've ever tasted."

My eyes flick to her mouth as she picks up a stalk of asparagus, slipping it between her lips. I close my eyes tightly as images of my cock slipping between her lips as she circles her tongue around the tip fill my mind. I grip the edge of the table, barely hanging on to my control.

"I'm glad you're enjoying it," I reply gruffly before digging into my food, trying not to imagine eating this off her before feasting on her pussy for dessert. After a few moments, I get my body under some sort of control, and we fall into easy conversation.

Audrey asks about my business and about growing up here in Tyson's Creek. She seems fascinated about living in a small town where everyone is there for each other when we need them. I explain to her how almost the entire town rallied around me when Lydia passed away, even people I had never met before. The outpouring of love was unlike anything I'd ever experienced. Audrey and Love have spent so much time alone, with no one to truly depend on, that having an entire town to help you seems like a foreign concept.

We both laugh at my stories about the trouble Vance and I used to get into when we were younger. I don't shy away from telling stories that involve Lydia, wanting Audrey to know the woman she was. She doesn't complain once, wanting to know everything she can about her and some of our friends were growing up. I would've expected her to not want to hear about anything involving Lydia, but she seems to really understand how much Lydia meant to me and how she will always be a part of Jade's and my life.

"Why me?" Audrey asks, taking a sip of her wine. "Out of all the women you could've dated over the years, why me?"

"Would you believe me if I said that the moment I laid eyes on you, I knew you were special?"

"Maybe." She giggles, blushing slightly.

"Well, it's true." I take a moment to collect my thoughts before taking a sip of my beer. "I was swept off my feet the moment I laid eyes on you. It was as if at that moment, the world stopped spinning, and we were the only two people in it."

I reach down and grab her hand, giving it a small squeeze. "It was as if the universe sent you and Love to me so that I knew what I was missing in my life."

"Me and Love?"

"Yes, both of you." Tears pool in her eyes as I

continue speaking. "It's always been Jade and me against the world, but you and Love complete us in a way we didn't know we needed. We all balance each other. Where Love is quiet and thinks things through, Jade is impulsive and tends to be in your face with everything."

Audrey snickers softly, wiping her cheek quickly. "But there's nothing wrong with that. She is the person she was meant to be. How can anyone help but love her?"

"Exactly. And how can anyone help but be attracted to you two?" I need to ensure she understands what she and Love mean to us.

A glimmer of pain crosses her face, disappearing just as quickly. "I would love to believe you, but I can't shake the feeling that this is all just a dream. That, at some point, I'll wake up with my heart shattered into a million pieces."

"I'd never do anything to intentionally hurt you, Audrey."

"I'd love to say I know that, but how do I know you aren't lying? How do I know that you'll really love me and my daughter, no matter what?"

I lean forward, brushing my thumb across her cheek. "What happened, Audrey?" She leans into my palm, her eyes drifting closed. "It seems like Ian hurt you deeply, both you and Love. Now you're too afraid to trust someone with your heart again."

"Ian, I assume the girls told you." Not a question, but a statement. A single tear trickles down her cheek a she pulls her hand from my grasp. I notice her hands shaking slightly before they disappear below the table and are out of sight.

"I met him at work, teaching yoga at a small studio in Dallas. He asked me to go to dinner a few times, but I said no. I did everything I could to convince him not to go out with me, but he persisted. After a few months, he asked me for coffee. I figured I would humor him, hoping he would stop asking, but that's not how things turned out."

She sighs loudly, her shoulders rolling in on themselves, as if she is trying to disappear. "He was charming and compassionate. He didn't judge me for being a single mother, and after a few months of dating, I let him meet Love."

I reach for her hand again and thread our fingers together, giving her the strength to continue her story. "Once Love gave her seal of approval, things moved quickly. After almost a year of dating, we moved into his place in the city." Audrey swipes at the tears streaming down her cheeks, throws her shoulders back, and straightens her back. "Everything was amazing, until it wasn't. I thought he loved me and was planning to marry me and make us a real family, but he already had one of those."

"What do you mean?"

"Ian was already married. He had a wife and two kids who lived on the East Coast."

"Motherfucker." My hands ball into fists on the top of the table as rage slowly fills my body. I want to lash out and break something, anything, to sate the anger burning through my veins. "If I ever get my hands on him, I'll..."

"No matter how badly I want to let you beat the crap out of him, it won't change anything." Audrey places her hand on top of mine, her thumb rubbing small circles across my skin. "When I confronted him about it, he scoffed. The trips he was taking for work back to the East Coast were when he was with his real family.

"I knew I needed to put as much space as I could between Ian and us. Bristol had been begging me to move here since she opened her yoga studio a few years ago, so I finally took her up on her offer."

I clench my eyes tightly and inhale deeply, trying to purge the rage inside me. It takes a few moments, but I get my emotions back under control. "I'm sorry."

"You did nothing wrong, Connor. I'm flattered you were so angry on our behalf.

"So, that's why I can't believe a word you say, Connor. I can't risk ruining things for Love and me again. We finally have a place to call home, the family we've been missing since my parents died. I don't want to do anything to jeopardize that."

"Can't that family include Jade and me?" I whisper as I get up from my seat and kneel next to her, cupping her cheek with my hand. Audrey closes her eyes and nuzzles into my palm. "The part of myself I lost when Lydia died has finally found its way back to me. It's all because of you, Audrey."

The primal urge to claim her is replaced by the desire

to care for her and Love, to give them everything they deserve. I gently brush my lips against hers, and when she doesn't respond, I do it again, but with more force this time. Her lips move against mine until I slide the tip of my tongue against them, begging for entrance. Audrey parts her lips slightly, and I devour her mouth with my own, putting all my feelings into this kiss, wanting to show her how much she has come to mean to me in such a short amount of time.

We break apart, gasping for air, and I rest my forehead against hers. "Audrey, when are you going to understand how much you two mean to me?" I say, our eyes locking with each other. "Let me love you," I beg, waiting for her to give me a signal that she is ready to become mine. "Let me take care of you. Of both of you."

"Show me, Connor. Show me what it means to be loved by you." She places a gentle kiss on the tip of my nose as I push my arm underneath her legs and wrap the other around her shoulders, lifting her into my arms. I grimace slightly as pain shoots down my back but stand quickly and stride toward the stairs, taking them two at a time. "I can walk, you know." Audrey laughs before burying her nose into my chest.

"Oh, that's one of my favorite sounds in the world." I sigh, relief coursing through my body at the sound of her joy.

I plant a kiss on her forehead before heading into my room and shutting the door. I send up a silent prayer of thanks that the girls are not here. Making love to Audrey with two teenage girls a few doors down is something I'll have to get used to, but right now, I want to hear her scream my name, completely uninhibited and at my mercy, which could only happen if the girls aren't here.

I drop her onto the bed with a bounce before crawling over her, pinning her in place with my body. "Everything will change after this, Audrey. If you want to stop, just let me know."

She licks her lips and leans forward, gripping my ear between her teeth. I groan and grind my cock into her stomach.

"Yes," is the only thing she says as my hand snakes between us toward the button of her jeans. Unfastening her pants, I lean back on my knees and pull them down her legs, tossing them to the floor. Spreading her legs wide, I settle between them and run my nose up her slit. "I've been dying to get a taste of your pussy."

"What are you waiting for?" she questions as I pull her panties to the side, locking eyes with her as I lick her pussy.

"You taste like sunshine and honey, like everything good in the world." I groan as I plunge my tongue between her folds. Her essence floods my mouth as I suck on her clit, desperate to get every drop into my mouth.

"Oh, god," she moans, biting down on her lip to keep quiet. "I've never..." Her words trail off as I delve a finger inside her. "It's never felt like this before."

"And it never will with anyone else. Don't you feel it,

Audrey?" I grind my cock into the mattress and groan before inserting a second finger inside her.

"Yes," she whispers, threading her fingers through my hair and tugging lightly. "Don't stop. Please, don't stop."

"So fucking tight, gorgeous. I could stay between your legs forever." She arches off the bed, and I use my other arm to hold her in place.

Her pussy tightens around my tongue as she climbs higher and higher toward release. I find her G-spot with my finger and caress it. "Come for me. Give me everything."

I latch on to her clit once again and suck, sending her flying over the edge as she moans my name. I continue to nibble and lick her as she comes back down to earth. Pulling my fingers out of her pussy, I shove them into my mouth and lick them clean.

I stand and unfasten my jeans, pushing them down and stepping out of them. Locking eyes with Audrey, I push my boxers to the floor, as well, and my cock springs free. Audrey licks her lips in anticipation as she lifts to her knees and grips my cock with her hands.

fifteen

audrey

I lean forward and wrap my hand around his cock, pulling him toward me. His lightly tanned skin feels smooth against my hand as I pump my hand up and down his shaft, collecting precum in my hand with each pass.

"Audrey," Connor moans as I run my tongue down the length of his cock. "Stop."

I freeze in place, resting back on my heels. "What's the matter? Don't you..." My voice trails off, not sure how to ask if he wants me to suck his dick.

"No. This isn't about me," he whispers as I release him. "Let me show you how much you mean to me."

Connor leans forward and captures my lips with his before leaning back slightly. "Just let me show you how I'm falling in love with you."

I gasp in surprise as we stare at each other. Connor's eyes are full of desire, as expected. But behind the desire, I see something else—love. And that terrifies me. Connor Bennett is everything I've ever wanted in a partner. He cares about me, his friends, his family, and most importantly, my daughter. But that nagging voice in the back of my head keeps telling me not to trust whatever this is. I believe Ian loved me, that I was the only person in his heart, but I was just a replacement for the wife he had on the other side of the country. Connor will always love Lydia. He's never denied that, but can he love me, too? Is there room in his heart for Love and me or will he just see me as a replacement for the love he lost?

"What are you thinking about so hard?" Connor's fingertips dig into my waist, holding me against him like he's afraid I'll disappear.

We stare at each other for a few moments. I try to make sense of all these swirling emotions running through my mind. I want to tell him everything, all my fears, and lay them at his feet and beg him to make all the doubts disappear, but my mind keeps screaming that it isn't possible.

"Stop thinking so much," Connor whispers, brushing his lips against my forehead. "Just feel, Audrey."

Electricity pulses in my veins, turning into a burning need as one of his hands slips beneath my shirt. His calloused fingers brush against my nipples as he wraps his hand around my breast and squeezes. The heat of his palm against my skin brings a moan from my mouth.

"Are you okay?" He kneels on the bed, pushing on my shoulder gently.

A shiver runs through my body as I stroke his cock, precum leaking from the tip onto my hand. I nod my head, unable to form words.

"I haven't been with anyone in years." His voice caresses my skin, causing goosebumps to pebble on my flesh. "I want you more than anything, but I don't have any condoms."

"It's okay," I whisper against his lips before nibbling on his bottom lip. "I'm on birth control and got tested after I found out about Ian's wife."

"Thank fuck." He groans as his finger brushes against my clit, rubbing small circles on the sensitive bundle of nerves between my legs.

I shut my eyes tightly as his fingers slip between my folds, gently pulling them out before slowly sliding them back in. My eyes roll into the back of my head as I teeter on the edge of an explosive orgasm, embarrassingly fast. I whimper softly as heat crawls up my neck.

"Imagine this is my cock and come for me." Connor curls his fingers slightly, hitting my G-spot for the second time before capturing my lips with his, swallowing my moan of pleasure.

My chest rises and falls quickly as his other hand grips my breast, manipulating my body like his own personal plaything. He leans forward, and the heel of his palm grinds down hard on my clit, causing my legs to tremble. My hips ride his hand, both desperate to come and aching for him to be inside me.

"Come for me." His breath fans against my ear before the sharp sting of his teeth on my neck pushes me over the edge into oblivion. Blinding white euphoria explodes behind my eyes, and a strangled cry bounces off the walls, letting anyone within shouting distance know what just happened between us.

I don't even have time to come down from my orgasm before Connor pulls his fingers out and replaces them with his cock. "I feel so full." I moan as he gently pulls out and thrusts back in.

Connor takes my mouth in an aggressive kiss, the salty tang I now taste informing me he sucked my cum off his fingers. His hand trails down my leg, wrapping one around his waist as I slowly lift the other and wrap it around him. His cock slides in even deeper as he grips my ass and thrusts.

"I never..." I moan, my eyes clenching shut as arousal races through my body.

Every nerve ending in my body feels as if it's on fire, climbing towards an impossible end. Higher and higher, clenching so hard around the intrusion that's controlling every aspect of my life at this moment.

"I know," he responds, his arms bulging as he fights to maintain control.

I've never felt so cherished by a man before, but right now, I need Connor in a way I can't put into words. "I don't need slow and sweet. Fuck me, Connor."

"I don't want to hurt you," he gets out between clenched teeth.

"Give me all of you, Connor. No holding back." That's all it takes for him to let loose and begin pounding my pussy into submission.

My mind can no longer process words, only feelings.

The way the stubble of his cheek brushes against my cheek. The slight twinge of pain as his fingertips dig into my skin as he pounds into me. The slapping sound of our skin as he brings me closer to oblivion. The sound of my breath as I'm panting, begging for him to give me what I need.

"Please. Please. Please," I beg, unable to think of anything but the inevitable euphoria of my release.

"Come with me, Audrey." He groans as his hand slides between us, pinching my clit between his two fingers. His thrusts become erratic, losing the smooth glide he had. "Come now."

Connor roars, slamming into me only twice more before stilling, his seed spilling deep inside of me. I scream his name loudly, every muscle in my body constricting as indescribable pleasure shoots through my body.

Connor slows his pace, pumping in and out of me to draw out my orgasm. Tiny aftershocks course through my body as he rolls to the side and slides out of me with a groan. I lay my head gently on his chest as he pulls the covers up and over us. My lungs can't pull in enough air. I can barely hear anything over the sound of my heart pounding in my ears, but I am acutely aware of him. I hiss when he pulls back, his softening cock dragging against my sensitive flesh.

"You're mine, Audrey," he whispers into the darkness. "You know that, don't you?" Connor plants a kiss on my shoulder, snuggling his body tightly against mine.

There are a million things I should say that he needs

to know, but I can't. Fuck. Fuck. I should never have allowed this to happen, to let him this close to my heart. He probably still loves his wife because there's no way this can be happening to me. I'm always careful and patient before getting into a relationship, but with Connor, I'm falling back into bad habits. I took my time with Ian, and look where that got me. Connor is going to break my heart, just like Trey and Ian did, but this time, I know I won't survive.

Tears pool in my eyes as I try to force myself to go to sleep. I need time to think this through, to process everything that happened tonight, and to ask the powers that be what to do next. I can't be trusted to decide on my own, especially on something this important.

"Go to sleep, Connor. I'm sure the girls will be calling early in the morning to find out how our date went."

Don't leave me. Please, don't leave me.

"I'm not going anywhere." His chest rumbles as I freeze, completely unaware that I was saying anything aloud.

"You can't promise," I whisper, and my eyes drift shut as the weight of the last few hours come crashing down on me.

I feel Connor's lips brush against my forehead before he whispers in my ear. "This is one promise I know in my soul I'll keep."

As I drift off, I hope that when I wake up in the morning, everything will be as it should be and that I haven't set myself up for heartbreak once again.

I feel like it's only a few minutes later when I bolt up straight in the bed, clutching my chest, right over my heart, and look around the room. The soft glow of the morning sun filters through the window. Small shadows play across the wall from the trees outside.

"It must be just before sunrise," I say softly, catching sight of the pile of clothes at the foot of the bed.

"It's too early to be awake." Connor groans from beside me, throwing his arm across my waist and attempting to pull me back into the bed.

"I have to go to the bathroom," I whisper as I remove his arm and slide out of the bed, pulling the blanket with me.

You weren't this shy last night when his face was intimately acquainted with your pussy.

"I've already seen everything before and have plans of tracing every inch of you with my tongue when you come back to bed."

My cheeks heat with embarrassment as I clutch the blanket tightly to my body, memories of what happened filling my mind. I scoop my clothes off the floor and scurry to the bathroom, the deep baritone of Connor's voice following behind me.

"What was I thinking?" I say to my reflection, turning on the faucet and splashing cool water onto my face.

I wasn't thinking, that's the problem. I let my feelings for Connor and the way he made my body sing dictate my actions, letting my emotions be in control. The exact opposite of what I should have done. "I need to get home so I can think without Connor near me."

I quickly slip back into my clothes before quietly opening the bathroom door and peeking out to see if Connor is still awake. By some stroke of luck, he's fallen back to sleep. The sheet is draped over his legs as the sunlight reflects against his tan, giving it a warm glow. My hand twitches at my side with the need to run the tips of my fingers down the planes of his chest, taking my time to trace each of his ab muscles as they flex beneath my fingers.

It wouldn't take much effort to strip down and return to bed, eagerness for a repeat performance of last night overcoming me, but I shake my head. I need to think this through and make sure that whatever this is between Connor and me is worth risking everything, and I can't do that wrapped in his arms.

"Trying to make a clean getaway?" I gasp in shock before spinning around and coming face-to-face with Connor. He's propped up in the bed, the sheet pooling around his waist.

"I need to head to work. Bristol called while I was in the bathroom and asked me to take over her class this morning," I choke out as he slides out of the bed, thankfully with a pair of boxers on, and wraps his arms around me.

"Hmm, too bad. I was really hoping to have you for breakfast." Connor nuzzles his nose into the crook of my neck and inhales deeply before planting a kiss on the shell of my ear.

"Sorry. Duty calls," I keep my head down as I try to slip out of his arms, but it's no use.

Connor grips my chin, forcing me to look at him. "Don't run away from me, okay? I'm sorry if I scared you with what I said last night, but I meant every word. I won't take them back, but I can wait for you to feel the same way. I'm not going anywhere."

"Okay." My voice cracks slightly, my sense of self-preservation telling me I need to run as far away from here as possible. "I'll call you later."

Connor's eyes scan my face, searching for any sign of a lie on my part, then leans forward and kisses me softly. "See you later, beautiful."

I nod my head quickly before spinning on my heels and heading down the stairs and straight out the front door. Searing pain flows through my entire body as waves of agony pull me under as I shut the front door behind me and race toward my car.

"I just need to hold on until I get home." I sob as I yearn for numbness to cut me off from all these feelings that I'm so desperate to forget.

I don't know how I get home and pull into my driveway, but I don't move. It could have been only a few minutes or an hour as I sit here, my head resting against the steering wheel, alternating between soul-crushing sobs and numbness. What started out as an amazing day with the promise of a happy ending has come crashing to the ground because I can't seem to stop worrying about the what-ifs.

"I can't believe this is happening again." I bury my face in my hands and continue to sob, trying to make sense of the last hour of my life.

I tried to be careful and protect my heart from Connor, but he broke down all my defenses, worming his way into my heart and becoming a part of me. A part that will remain broken until the day I die. He promised to give me everything I could ever imagine, but I was too afraid of being another replacement that I sabotaged us before we even got started.

The shrill ring of my cellphone in my back pocket breaks me from my stupor. "Hello."

"Hey, girl." Bristol's voice comes across the line. "The baby is not too happy this morning. Is there any way you can open the studio and teach the first class for me this morning?"

Tears pool in my eyes as all the emotions I've been trying desperately to keep in check come bubbling to the surface. "Bristol."

"What happened?"

"I messed up. I let him... I let him..." My heart constricts in my chest as the expectations of everyone come crashing down around me. I gasp for air as sadness unlike anything I've ever felt overtakes me.

"I'm coming over. Don't freaking move."

Tears pour down my cheeks as the weight of my feelings hit me. I clutch the phone tightly, biting down on my hand, hoping to quiet the sobs bubbling from my throat. My heart feels as if it's breaking in two. I want nothing more than to turn the car around, run into Connor's arms, and beg him to bind us together in every way possible.

Bristol makes it to me in no time and as she slides into the passenger seat I cry out, "Make it stop," I wrap my arms around my waist and attempt to hold myself together. "I just want the pain to stop."

"I wish I could." Bristol's voice fills the cab of my car as she wraps her arms around me. "I need you to tell me what happened."

"Connor told me he was falling in love with me." Tears stream down my face as I gasp for breath. "But how is that even possible?"

It was more than just sex between us, I know that, but how can I trust something that happened so quickly? Is it even possible to fall in love with someone this fast? It's only been a little over a month since we met. There are plenty of stories out there where people fall in love at first sight, but this is the real world. Happily ever afters aren't that easy. You have to work for them.

"Maybe the universe is trying to tell you something," she says. I slam my eyes shut, plunging myself into darkness.

"I doubt that." Fresh tears run down my cheeks as I pull out of Bristol's embrace and climb out of the car. "The universe loves to give me a taste of happiness before ripping it away. But this time, I won't let it happen."

"What the heck do you mean, Audrey?" Bristol slams my car door shut and follows me toward my front door.

"Connor is everything I could ever want in a man. He's kindhearted, attentive, and treats Love like she's his own child. He'd give someone the shirt off his back if they needed it, no questions asked."

"So, umm, what's the problem?"

"It's too good to be true. It's too soon. Take your pick!" My head shakes back and forth as I drop my chin to my chest, not wanting to see the sympathetic look in her eyes that I know is there. I inhale a deep breath and let it out slowly, attempting to calm my emotions. "I've been a replacement for someone before. I won't let that happen again. I deserve more and so does Love."

"You aren't making any sense, Audrey."

"I am. There's no way he loves me. He's just looking for a replacement for Lydia. That's all this is, and as soon as I let my guard down, he's going to leave me."

I'm nothing special, I repeat in my mind as I open my front door and head inside. Everything looks exactly like I left it and where it belongs, but somehow, it feels different.

"I couldn't handle that, so I need to figure out how to end things before he breaks my heart." I feel a sob bubbling up in my chest, threatening to escape from my mouth.

"You're a fucking idiot." Bristol wraps her arm around my shoulders, leading me toward the couch. "Did you ever stop to think that maybe you've finally found what you've been searching for?"

"Maybe." I sniffle, not wanting to burst into tears again. "But what if I make the wrong decision? Then the life Love and I have started building here will end."

"And you could get struck by lightning the moment you step out your front door."

"Be serious."

"I am." Bristol brushes a few strands of hair off my face. "You never know what life will bring. The only thing we can do is put one foot in front of the other and keep living. So, what's the problem with having a relationship with Connor?"

I freeze, not knowing exactly how to answer her question. Tears stream down my face as I gasp for breath. "But what if things don't work out?"

"Then you call us, and we'll figure it out. Nothing a few pints of ice cream and a stack of chick flicks can't cure."

Bristol and I sit there in silence as I think about what she said. I need to be honest with myself. I'm falling in love with Connor. I may not be ready to jump into a relationship with him, but the feelings are there. Maybe they've always been there, growing into something beautiful, perfect, and beyond anything I could ever imagine. I wasn't searching for forever when I moved here, but it seems it may have fallen into my lap.

"My work here is done," Bristol says suddenly before planting a kiss on my cheek and struggling to get off my couch. "Since you are obviously in no condition to teach class, I'm going to head in."

"No, I'll come in." My chest tightens as I panic. I need some place to hide and think alone. None of them will bother me if they know I'm working. "Please," I beg.

"Okay. But for the record, I think this is a bad idea." Bristol eyes me skeptically before waddling toward my front door. "I'll see you soon."

"Thank you," I croak before scurrying up the stairs to take a shower. I turn on the shower and strip off my clothes. As the bathroom fills with steam, I try to focus on anything but what happened between Connor and me last night. Either way, I need to figure out what I want in this situation because it's not fair to either of us.

Maybe I can ask the cards...

I hop into the shower and clean up. Not bothering to wash my hair, I shut the water off and step out, wrapping a towel around myself. Ignoring my reflection, I reach into my top drawer and grab underwear and, at the last minute, my deck of tarot cards. I place the deck on the top of my dresser, drop my towel, and step into my underwear.

"What's the worst that the cards could say?" I whisper into my empty room as I shove my arms through the straps and pull the bra over my head.

That a relationship with Connor is a lousy idea.

I plop down on the edge of the bed, threading my arms through my sports bra and pulling it over my head before checking my reflection in the mirror above my dresser. My curls are a rumpled mess, sticking out in every direction like a haystack, but what gets my attention is my eyes. There is a life to them that hasn't been there in a while. Maybe this thing with Connor is a good thing. I've never been afraid of what the cards have to tell me. Why should I start now?

I push off the bed and head directly for the deck of tarot cards. I shuffled them last night before putting them in the drawer, so I don't bother doing it again. I take a deep breath to center myself before cutting the deck and shutting my eyes. I take one final cleansing breath and ask my question. "Is Connor trying to replace his wife with me?"

I flip the top card over and open my eyes, looking directly into the mirror. It's the Devil card, the worst card to pull in a relationship draw. "I have my answer," I whisper as tears fall down my cheeks like waterfalls. "There is no way I can have a healthy relationship with Connor Bennett."

I drop the rest of the deck as I pull out a random drawer and grab some clothes. I have no idea what I'm wearing, but it's better than going into public naked. Functioning on autopilot, I stumble out of my bedroom and down the stairs, grabbing my bag and yoga mat before heading out the door.

"He isn't over Lydia." My knuckles turn white as sadness turns to anger. That's the most logical conclusion when the Devil card appears. He's never hidden his feelings for his wife from me. At first, I thought it was to put me at ease, but maybe I was wrong. While I was baring my soul to him about what happened with Ian, the only thing he was interested in was a quick roll in the hay. My anger continues to bubble beneath the surface as I pull into a parking spot. He said all the right things to get me into bed with him, but I won't fall for that again. I refuse to be another replacement, a placeholder to bide their time while they love someone else.

"What happened?" Bristol's voice startles me as she knocks on the window, causing me to jump in surprise. "You were close to tears when I left your place, and now you look as if you're ready to commit murder."

I open the door and growl, "I fell for his tricks," before storming past her and into the studio. Heading directly for the break room, I throw my bag onto the table and pace. "I can't believe that even after I told him everything that happened with Ian, he still went through with his plan."

Bristol stands in my path. "You need to give me more information because you aren't making any sense."

I cross my arms over my chest. "After you left, I did a card reading to help me decide what to do..." I trail off as Bristol rolls her eyes at me.

"When are you going to stop basing your fate on those damn tarot cards?"

"I ignored the cards before with Ian. I can't make the same mistake again," I mumble. "I got the Devil card."

"And? That's what made you believe Connor was a complete asshole?" Bristol brushes past me and grabs a bottle of water from the cooler, quickly twisting off the cap and taking a swig. "Connor is the best thing that has ever happened to you and Love. Don't let some stupid cards get in the way of your happiness."

I lean against the door frame and think about everything Bristol said. I'm letting my attachment to those cards get in the way again. Connor is a devoted father and has been nothing but truthful with me since I arrived in town. If the rumor mill in town is correct, Connor hasn't been with anyone since Lydia died, only me. There's no way he was intentionally leading me on, but the cards still say we aren't meant to be together.

"You're right. There's no way Connor would use me, but we can't be together."

"Why is that?" Bristol grabs my hand, pulling me to sit at the small table in the break room.

"He wants a relationship, and that's not something I can give him right now. I need to focus on Love. If something were to go wrong between us, I don't want to uproot her again."

"Ugh. This conversation is like beating a dead horse. You need to stop worrying about the things that could go wrong. Why not focus on what could go right?" Bristol laughs. "There hasn't been one person who has caught his eye in fourteen years but you. If that isn't a sign from the universe, I don't know what is."

"I need to focus on Love," I affirm one last time before we hear the bell chime, signaling someone has arrived. "I have a class to teach."

"No, you have a class to *take*. You need to spend some quality time with yourself." Bristol pats my hand before rising from her seat and heading toward the front.

I wish I could find some way for us to have a happy ending, but the cards never lie. I need to end this before either of us gets in too deep. I don't know if I can survive another heartbreak. The one thing I know is I need to make a clean break between Connor and me. We have Jade and Love to think about. I need to end this sooner rather than later to ensure we can at least be civil with each other.

I know what I need to do, but why does my heart feel like it's breaking into a million pieces? Heartbreak is something I've become accustomed to over the last few years, but right now, all I feel is soul-wrenching pain at the thought of things changing between Connor and me.

sixteen

connor

I toss and turn for a few minutes after Audrey leaves before climbing out of bed to start my day. I head directly for my dresser to grab some clean clothes, glimpsing my wedding ring sitting on the top of it.

"Hey, Lyds," I whisper, picking up the ring and wrapping it in my hand. "I haven't done this in a long time, but I want to make sure you understand."

I don't know many people who sit down and talk to the dead, but for me, it's a comfort. I tell Lydia about every major event in our lives. When Jade walked for the first time, when Vance and I had our first successful year in the business, when Selina came back to town. I know she's looking down on us.

"I love her." My eyes drift shut as I fight to maintain control of my emotions. "I never believed it would be possible for me to love someone again, but here we are."

This is the first time I've said those three words out loud about anyone but Jade in over a decade. It seems wrong coming from my lips, especially when speaking to my deceased wife, but this is something I need to do for myself. To ensure that the universe knows how deeply I love Audrey and my wife at the same time.

"I still love you, Lyds. I always will, and Audrey knows that. But my love for her is different. I love her as strongly and as deeply as you, but..." My voice trails off, trying to find the words to explain.

The cool metal of the ring warms in my hand as I tighten my grip and drop onto the edge of my bed.

"Our love was all-consuming, Lyds. You were the air that I breathed. My soulmate. And when you died, I was lost. A shell of the man I once was. I wanted to crawl into that hole and die right along with you, but I couldn't. I had our little girl to take care of, a tiny piece of you that would remain by my side until I took my last breath."

Tears stream down my cheeks as I clutch the ring tighter in my hand, placing it over my heart. The sadness of that time in my life swirls around me, threatening to pull me under, but I continue.

"I put one foot in front of the other for our little girl, giving her anything and everything she could want, while also closing myself off from the world. I went through the motions for those around me, appearing happy and thriving to stave off their concerns, but in reality, I was dead inside. My soul was missing, enveloping me in darkness. I was content to live like that for the rest of my life, holding on to the hope that I'd find you after my dying breath."

Bitterness courses through my veins that fate could be so cruel. Lydia and I had planned to have a life together, to grow old together, but the universe had other plans. I had wanted to rage against the world and make anyone pay for the pain I was dealing with, but that wouldn't change anything. I had a little girl to take care of. That was my life's purpose from that moment forward. I didn't have space in my life for love, companionship, or passion, so I closed off that part of myself, deciding that Jade was the only thing I needed in life... until I met Audrey and realized we both deserved more.

"But when Audrey arrived in town, her light shone into the recesses of my heart. The moment I saw her, it awoke my once-dormant heart. At first, I was afraid that even starting a relationship with her would mean I had to abandon my love for you, but I slowly realized there was room in my heart for both of you. Our love was all-consuming, but my love for Audrey is like a healing balm, filling that part of my heart that went missing when you died."

I was caught completely off guard when I saw her sitting alone in Just the Drip a little over a month ago. I knew then that she was special, but I never could have imagined things turning out like this. That she would come to mean so much to me after only a month. It sounds insane, but I know deep in my heart that Audrey is it for me. She understands me in a way that no one else has in over a decade. She and Love soothe the ache that has remained in my heart since Lydia passed. Audrey has given me a companion, someone to love besides my daughter. Love has given Jade a best friend, the sibling she's always wanted. Neither of them will ever replace Lydia in our hearts, but they can help it ache a little less, giving us back the part of ourselves that was missing.

"Thank you for sending her here. To Jade and me. We need Audrey and her daughter, Love. Just like they need us," I say with conviction as I push off the bed and stroll toward the door.

I haven't worn my wedding ring since the night Audrey, Love, Jade, and I had dinner. It was the first time in years that it felt like it was weighing me down instead of keeping me anchored to this world. I debated for hours whether I should do it, but the moment I removed it from its resting place, I felt a sense of peace.

I pull open the top drawer of my dresser, reaching to grab the small red bag tucked under some socks in the corner. When Lydia was being wheeled into surgery, they made her take off all her jewelry, including her wedding and engagement rings. I knew that she'd want to give these to Jade when she was older, so I didn't bury her with them.

"I'll always love you, Lyds, but it's time for me to look forward instead of backward," I whisper as I place the ring into the small bag along with Lydia's engagement and wedding rings and put it back into the drawer before pushing it shut. I stand there in silence for a few moments, my hand still resting on the drawer, and sigh loudly. The same sense of peace I felt when I removed my ring fills my heart, letting me know deep down in my soul that Lydia is okay with my decision to move on.

"Goodbye, Lyds," I say with conviction as I turn toward the bathroom to hop into the shower.

My body moves on autopilot as I take a shower, wanting to see Audrey immediately. I told her I was falling in love with her last night, which probably scared her. But the need to be near her is almost unbearable. Although I know in my heart we're meant to be together, she may still have some reservations. I just need to be patient with Audrey, giving her time to process all the big emotions I dropped into her lap last night. However, that's much easier said than done.

I climb out of the shower and get dressed quickly. Audrey said she had to teach a class for Bristol this morning, but that doesn't mean I can't take her to lunch or something between classes. The girls are having a sleepover with Vance, so I doubt I'll see either of them before noon. I need to find something to keep me occupied. Most men would plop down on the couch and watch some television, but I need to stay busy.

"I should eat something," I mutter to myself as I head down the stairs and into the kitchen to make myself something to eat.

I grab some eggs and bacon out of the fridge and make myself a breakfast sandwich.

If things had gone according to plan, I'd be delivering this breakfast to Audrey in bed before having her for dessert, but there was something off when she left this morning.

While I eat, I replay in my mind everything that

happened this morning like a movie reel. I focus on the tears I noticed pooling in her eyes as she said goodbye, the way her hands were shaking slightly when she placed them on my chest, and the break in her voice when she said goodbye. There was a tone of finality to our conversation that I didn't notice until now. My heart aches in my chest at the thought of things ending between us.

"Everything is fine. Besides, she said she would call me later," I mumble as I finish my breakfast and place the plate in the dishwasher. "Man, I really should clean this place up before the girls get home."

Home. It seems like such a small thing to think, but this is our home. A place for our little family to grow closer to each other. Lydia and I bought this place together, but having Audrey and Love live here with us will finally make it feel like a home.

"Don't get ahead of yourself, Connor." I chuckle darkly as I head into the dining room.

It seems in my haste to show Audrey how loved and cherished she was, I left our dinner and plates on the table. I make quick work of clearing the table and loading the dishes into the dishwasher. While the dishwasher is running, I wipe down all the countertops in the kitchen before sweeping and mopping the floor. It doesn't take long, but once I'm satisfied, I check my phone to make sure it's charged. I'm not sure if I put it on the charger before Audrey and I got carried away last night.

Double-checking to see if it has a full charge, I head to my room to plug it in, just in case. Since I'm already here, I tackle my room. I grab all the dirty laundry splayed over the floor and pull the sheets off the bed. Audrey's scent and memories of our night together come flying back into my mind.

What passed between us was real. It's only natural she's afraid to commit to another relationship so soon. The anger I felt last night at her confession about Ian bubbles under the surface as I pull in a deep breath. Ian should be shot for what he did to Audrey, Love, and his wife. No one deserves to be treated as if they could be easily discarded and replaced without a second thought.

I feel a pang in my heart at the idea of Audrey feeling that way. Is that why she ran away from me this morning? I've never hidden anything from her. Audrey knows I was married before and that I have no intention of replacing my dead wife with her. She has to know that my feelings are real, that she's the only woman I can imagine loving.

Shoving all the laundry into the hamper, I pull out a fresh set of sheets from the linen closet and remake my bed. Once that's finished, I take it one step further and dust every surface I can think of until it sparkles.

"The next time Audrey comes to visit, there won't be a dust bunny in sight," I say out loud. I check my phone again for any missed calls or messages.

"You aren't a teenager anymore. If you want to talk to her, you should call her. There is no rule that says you can't call her." I should stop talking to myself, but I'm out of practice. I have no idea what the new rules are for dating someone, but I may just lose my mind if I keep going like this. Nothing says I have to sit here and wait for Audrey to call me.

It's been a little over four hours since she left my house this morning. A perfectly reasonable amount of time to wait before calling to see how she is doing. Yoga classes only last an hour or so, and if she's busy, I can just leave her a message.

Suddenly, my phone vibrates in my hand, startling me. I juggle the phone in my hand a few times before finally glimpsing the number on the screen.

"Hey, Squirt. You're up early." I smile. A pang of disappointment passes through me that it's not Audrey calling.

"Hey, Dad. How are you?"

"Fine. How are you?"

"Fine."

"Is that all you called for, or is there something else you want to ask?" I chuckle, plopping down on the end of my bed.

We sit in silence for a few minutes, waiting for the other to speak before Jade breaks the silence.

"Fine. Is it okay for us to come home yet? Uncle Vance said that you and Audrey might be getting busy."

The fuck? I'm going to need to have a conversation with my best friend. But he isn't wrong. If Audrey hadn't gone to work, there's no telling what state of undress we'd be in right now. The last thing we'd want is to be caught by one or both of our girls.

"Not that it's any of your business, but you can come

home whenever you want. Audrey went to Nurture Space to teach a class for Bristol this morning."

"Great. Uncle Vance will bring us back to the house now."

"Okay, see you soon. Love you."

"Love you, too, Dad."

I quickly hang up and stare at my phone. Audrey probably would want to know where Love is, right? I doubt she would have texted her early this morning, knowing how much her daughter loves her sleep. I should call her to let her know our plans. At least that's what I'm going with.

I dial her number and wait for an answer. Unfortunately, it goes right to voicemail. I debate about hanging up but leave a voicemail just to let her know what's going on and that I am thinking about her.

"Hey! If you hear this message, I'm teaching a class or ignoring you. I'll call you back when I can if I want to speak to you. Bye." Audrey's beautiful voice cuts off right before the tone.

"Hey, beautiful! Just wanted to hear your voice. I know it sounds lame, but it's the truth. Don't worry about Love. Vance is bringing the girls back to my house. If you could shoot me a text and let me know what the game plan is, I'd appreciate it. Oh, and I miss you. Bye."

"Really smooth there." I chuckle as I hang up the phone, hoping now that I've heard her voice, I can stop obsessing over everything.

I grab my laundry basket and figure it's time to get

the laundry done. The pile is almost as big as I am. Might as well get a head start on it. I'm heading back downstairs toward the laundry room when both girls come barreling through the front door.

I don't even have time to brace myself as both girls slam into me, one on each side, wrapping their arms tightly around my waist. I drop the basket and wrap my arms around their shoulders, planting kisses on the top of their heads.

"Were you sitting in the driveway when you called?"

"Not exactly, but we were already halfway here when I thought about checking first." Vance chuckles, rubbing the back of his neck.

"Thanks for taking the girls last night."

"Anytime. I love spending time with my nieces."

Love pulls back slightly, her eyes widening in surprise as she looks at Vance. "Nieces?"

"Yes, nieces. You're part of the family now. Remember? Fungus." Jade releases her grip around my waist and reaches for Love's hand, giving it a small squeeze.

"Yup. Fungus," she whispers, burying her nose in my side.

"Hey, Squirt. I'm starving. Why don't we go see what your dad has to eat in this place?" Vance says, motioning his head toward Love.

"Sure," Jade replies, her eyebrows pulled down in concern as she releases her grip around my waist and follows her uncle into the kitchen.

"Hey, Little Bit. What's got you so upset suddenly?"

I turn in her embrace, wrapping both my arms around her and pulling her against my chest. I rest my cheek on the top of her head as her shoulders shake lightly. She doesn't make a sound, but I know that she's upset.

Although Love and I haven't spent much time alone together, I've learned a lot about her. She's quiet and reserved, spending most of her time ensuring that the people around her are happy instead of processing her own feelings. Audrey always says that Love has a good head on her shoulders and is more mature than kids her age, but I think deep down Love has been waiting for a place to belong.

"It's been just me and my mom for so long. It's a little hard for me to wrap my mind around the fact that I have so much more now," Love whispers as her arms tighten around my waist. "Do you love my mom?"

"I love both of you very much."

"I love you. You and Jade. Auntie Bristol, Selina, and Leia. I love going to Just the Drip with my mom and dance classes with Jade. I love Vance, even though he's more of a child than I am most of the time."

"And they love you, too. Nothing is ever going to change that."

Love pulls back slightly, tears streaming down her face. "My mom... she's been hurt badly in the past. She's so scared of it happening again that she might push you away, but can you promise you won't let her?"

"What do you mean?"

Love sighs loudly before taking a step back, wrapping her arms around her waist. “My mom is so scared of ruining the family we’ve built for ourselves by falling in love with you that she will find some way to convince herself this is a bad idea.”

She paces back and forth in the foyer, her shoulders hunched and her hands clasped in the center of her chest as she continues to speak. Love has been carrying the weight of the world on her shoulders until this moment. She wants to protect her mom, but she also wants to stop her from sabotaging something before it can even get started. A feeling I’m all too aware of.

“I’ve told her a million times that it’s okay to love you, but I’m not sure she’s listening to me. To her, my happiness is the most important thing in the world, sometimes even to the detriment of her own. Sure, she’s made a few bad decisions in the past, but she always puts me first.”

“Do you mean what happened with Ian?” Love nods her head slightly in the affirmative.

“Him and my dad. My mom loves with her whole heart, and sometimes it blows up in her face. I know my mom would never say she regrets I was born, but after what happened with Ian, I’m afraid she’s going to close herself off from finding the love she’s been searching so desperately for.”

Audrey hasn’t said much about Love’s biological father, but it seems they had a similarly unfulfilling relationship. Two men whom she loved deeply tossed her to the side like a piece of trash. No wonder she's terrified at the idea of starting a relationship with me, especially with the stakes being so much higher. Not only is Love's happiness at risk, but Jade's as well.

"That's understandable, Love. But your mom knows how I feel about her. I laid it all out for her last night."

"But did she tell you she loved you?"

I pause, thinking back through each of my conversations with Audrey last night. Not once did she outright say what her feelings were for me, but I didn't need her words. She showed me with every caress of her hand and touch of her lips against my skin. I know deep down that she's falling in love with me, maybe already *is* in love. I don't need her to say anything out loud.

"Not specifically, but..."

"That's a problem." Love throws her hands up in the air in defeat before striding towards me. She grips one of my hands tightly in hers, pulling me toward the door. "You need to go talk to my mom before it's too late."

"What do you mean, *too late*?" I recoil, pain shooting through my chest. When Audrey left this morning, I knew she was scared, but I never believed she would run away from me.

"Before she convinces herself that she doesn't love you."

"I'm not sure I understand what you're saying."

Love stops abruptly before releasing my hand and spinning on her heels to face me, her eyes locking with mine. "She has a deck of tarot cards that my grandmother gave to her. I think she believes she can't decide without asking them for guidance. Especially after everything that has happened. She says using them helps her, but I think she uses them as a crutch."

Love grips both of my hands with hers, her eyes filling with tears again as she pleads her case. "She asked them if you two should be in a relationship, and if I was a betting person, she probably went home and asked if the relationship was going to last."

I shake my head, unable to form the words. My heart feels like it's been ripped out of my chest, and it's only been a short amount of time. "What do I do?"

"Go find her. Now." Love gives my hands a final squeeze before taking a step back.

"Hey, Dad." Jade comes skidding back into the foyer. "Would it be okay if—" she begins but stops, noticing the tension in the room. "What's going on here?"

"Nothing much. Your dad just said he loves me and my mom. I truly believe that she's falling in love with him, too, but she's more than likely trying to stop loving him because she's afraid of breaking up our new family if something goes wrong," Love responds quickly, as if I wasn't even in the room.

"Oh, that's it?" Jade questions, her head swiveling between the two of us.

"No, there's more, but I figured the *Reader's Digest* version would work best for a situation like this."

"You thought right." Jade shoves her phone into her pocket before turning her attention toward me. "So, why are you still standing here? We'll never forgive you if we don't get our baby brother soon."

"Or sister. We wouldn't mind a sister either," Love chimes in, giggling softly.

"But what about you two? I can't just leave you here alone."

"Did you forget Uncle Vance is in the kitchen, stuffing his face?" Jade huffs. "Besides, we're fourteen, not five. Auntie Selina texted me to see if Love and I wanted to join a hip-hop class she's having today."

"Okay, grab your stuff. I can give you both a ride."

"Not necessary." Jade winks at me before bellowing her uncle's name. It only takes a few seconds before he appears in the doorway.

"You rang?" Vance questions as he winks at Love from across the room.

"You're taking both of us to the dance studio for hip-hop class while my dad goes to talk to Audrey."

"Did something happen?"

"Not yet, but he needs to get to my mom before she talks herself into doing something stupid and breaking all our hearts."

"Sounds serious."

"Very," Jade and Love say in unison.

"Okay, then. Do what you gotta do, Connor. I got our girls."

"Thanks, Vance."

"Anytime," he replies.

I give both girls a quick hug and shove my feet into

my boots before running out the door and hopping into my truck.

Downtown, I find a parking spot easily but am surprised to see Bristol standing outside the door. "I thought Audrey was covering your classes today?" I question as I shut off the car, a feeling of dread slowly creeping in.

"She was supposed to, but I was feeling better, so I came in."

"I'm glad." I can feel something is off, but I don't want to press her for any information.

"I see the wheels turning in your head, Connor. I know what happened, but I won't betray her confidence." Bristol grimaces. "Just be careful with her. She's been hurt so many times. I don't know if she knows what it's like to be cherished by someone."

"Love explained everything to me. I don't quite understand it all, but I'm hoping I'm not too late."

Bristol stares at me for a few moments before sighing loudly. "Honestly, I don't know. Good luck." She smiles as I stride past her.

I reach for the door and pull it open; the small bell chimes, signaling my arrival. Audrey is cleaning something in the back of the studio. "Hello, Audrey."

Her shoulders tense slightly, but she refuses to acknowledge my arrival. "Are you going to ignore me?" I wait a few moments, but still no answer.

Bristol's words from earlier filter into my mind.

Audrey is afraid of the emotions we shared last night. "Did you get my message from earlier?"

"Is there something wrong with Love? With Jade? Did something happen?" Her eyes widen as she drops the broom.

"Everything is fine, love," I stride toward her, wrapping her hands in mine. "I just wanted to know what the plan was for the rest of the day. Jade and Love made the executive decision that they're going to dance class at Selina's place this afternoon."

"Thank goodness." She sighs before pulling her hands from my grasp and picking up the broom to continue her cleaning.

"Why did you really leave this morning?"

"I told you, Bristol called because she was sick. Thanks for letting Love hang out at your house. I know she's a teenager, but I still worry about her being home alone," she replies, looking everywhere but into my eyes.

"It's no problem. I love having Love around." I grip her chin, forcing her to look into my eyes. "But don't avoid my question. Why did you leave, Audrey?" I stare into her eyes, willing her to see the feelings I did a horrible job of putting into words last night.

"I told you..."

"You need to do better than that, Audrey. I saw Bristol when I came in. She's perfectly fine." I thread my fingers through her hair, tugging her head back and exposing her neck to me.

"Tell me what I did wrong." I nibble down one side of her neck before making my way back up the other side. "Just tell me what to do so you understand how much I love you."

Tears spring to my eyes as I bury my nose in her neck, clinging to her body like it's an anchor holding both of us together. I rest my forehead against hers and speak from the heart. "Audrey, I barely existed before I saw you sitting in the coffee shop. You brought a light into my life that I didn't know was missing. Please, talk to me."

"I refuse to be your replacement for Lydia," she croaks, trying to wiggle out of my grasp, but I tighten my hold.

"You don't believe that, do you?" I lean back, cupping her cheeks in my palms. "I'd be lying if I said I didn't still love Lydia." I kiss the tip of her nose. "But there's room in my heart for both of you. I love you, Audrey."

"But it's too soon. Besides, you were still wearing your wedding ring until a few weeks ago. I'm just the first woman that's caught your attention." Audrey whimpers as she pulls away from me, her head swinging back and forth as she tries to process everything I've just dropped in her lap. Everything else fades into the background as she spins on her heels and dashes for the break room.

I should let her go, give her time, but I run after her and grasp her arm, spinning her around to face me. "Did the cards tell you something?"

Audrey recoils, as if I slapped her in the face. "How do you know about my cards?"

"Love told me." I take a step back from her, my arms dropping to the side. "She said you have a hard time trusting yourself to make decisions and use them as a buffer. But sometimes you see things in their answers that might not be there."

Love didn't say all of that, but I have a feeling I hit the nail on the head. "I don't know much about tarot cards, but I doubt they can tell the future."

"They don't, but they help point us in the right direction."

"And what did they say about me?"

"I'm not sure." She sobs, her entire body trembling as she turns her back toward me. "I think you should go."

I back away toward the door. I want to push her harder, to make her understand what she means to me, but I can't force her to see the truth. She needs space to process everything that I've said to her and to decide if being with me is worth it. Only she can make that decision for herself.

"Okay." I chuckle humorlessly as I continue backing away from her. "Please remember that I love you, and I'm willing to risk everything for a chance that you might love me in return."

She spins around, her hands reaching toward me as tears stream down her face. I want nothing more than to run to her, scoop her into my arms, and promise her that everything will be perfect between us, but I refuse to lie to her. Relationships are messy and take a lot of work. I can guarantee that we will disagree on something—heck, we'll even fight occasionally. But even when these things happen, I'll always love and protect her and Love.

I stride toward her, unable to resist the pull I feel in case this is the last time I set eyes on her. "This isn't the end of us, Audrey. Not by a long shot." I plant a kiss on the top of her head before turning on my heels and striding out the door, heading directly toward my truck.

Next thing I know, I'm pulling into my driveway, having no idea how I got home. I check the time, sending up a silent prayer of thanks that the girls aren't here. The last thing I want is to have them witness my world crumbling down around me.

Shutting off the car, I shoot Vance a quick text, asking him if he can pick up Jade from dance class. He replies instantly.

VANCE

The girls and I have a date with Selina. No need to worry about either of them. I gotcha covered for as long as you need.

CONNOR

You don't want a teenager tagging along on your date. Just bring Jade back here after class. You'll need to text Audrey about where she'd like Love to be dropped off.

VANCE

She isn't with you?

CONNOR

No.

I shake my head lightly before resting it on the seat, just taking time to think about what my life could be like without Audrey in it. It's only been a short time, but it feels like an eternity. Everything feels flat and lifeless now that things with the two of us are so up in the air. As far as I'm concerned, this isn't the end of the two of us, but how things proceed is up to Audrey.

Audrey was my chance at a new beginning. With that gone, what else is there to hope for? However, no matter what she decides, she and Love will be a part of our lives. No matter how badly it would hurt me to go back to the way things were, I'd do it for both of them. My happiness doesn't matter as long as my girls are happy. Everything will be okay.

seventeen

audrey

I don't know how I made it to the break room. The last thing I remember is the tiny bell over the door ringing, letting me know Connor had walked through it. I didn't have to turn around to know it was him. I could feel his presence the moment he arrived. It was like a beacon calling me home. I was powerless to resist. I should have bolted for the break room and hid from him, but that would've solved nothing.

Instead, I broke both our hearts. I keep telling myself that it was for the best, that I escaped with most of my heart intact, but even I know I'm full of shit. I'm teetering on the edge of an abyss. With one tiny push in either direction, I could be overcome by soul-crushing sobs or numbness at any moment. I stare at the door to the break room, waiting for Connor to appear, but he doesn't. Why would he after I told him to fuck off? Now, I'm left here alone to pick up the pieces of my broken heart, and I deserve it. I wanted to push him away before he could hurt me, and it worked, but now I'm an empty husk of the person I was before Connor and Jade came into my life.

"Things didn't go as well as you planned, did it?" Bristol asks as she comes strolling into the break room, taking a seat in an empty chair across from me. I scoff, unable to put into words how badly my conversation with Connor went.

"Love and Jade will be done with their hip-hop class soon. Vance and Selina offered to take the girls for a while tonight." Bristol reaches across the table, gripping my hand tightly. "Look at me, Audrey," she coaxes, but my eyes remain focused on the table in front of me.

I don't want to see the look of pity in her eyes that I know is there. I don't deserve her pity. I deserve this pain, the constant reminder of what could have been if things were different. Too bad they aren't. No matter how much my heart aches to be near Connor, I need to think about Love and what's best for her. If things didn't work out with Connor, we'd lose our newly formed family.

You've lost it anyway. I had hoped that we could go back to the way things were, but that's not possible. There's no way to stuff the all-encompassing love I felt—no, feel—for Connor.

"What happened, Audrey?"

I attempt to pull away, not ready to discuss what happened, but her grip tightens.

"I told him I didn't want to be a replacement for Lydia."

"You did what?" Bristol releases my hands, anger clear in her eyes. She takes a calming breath before speaking again. "How do you feel? Are you happy with the decision you made?"

"I feel like my heart has broken into a million pieces," I whisper, clutching at my chest. "But it doesn't matter how wrong this feels anymore."

"Oh, that's where you're wrong, Audrey. Tell me how you feel about Connor."

"I love him with all my heart." I gasp in surprise as the realization of my feelings hits me in full force.

Bristol places her hand on top of mine. "Then why are you doing this? If two people love each other, they can be together."

"But I asked my deck. I asked them if whatever this is between Connor and me would last, and it said no."

"Is that really what the cards said, or is that just what you wanted them to say?"

"It's not exactly what I asked, but it's not possible for me to manipulate the cards like that."

"Are you sure about that?" She pauses for a few seconds, waiting for me to rebut her statement, but when I don't respond, she continues. "Audrey, you're scared. You're afraid of being hurt by Connor. You're afraid of getting between Love's relationship with Jade. And most importantly, you're afraid of being wrong again. Is it possible that the cards are wrong?"

The cards can be wrong, but they never have been.

The problem is, I never listen. I've always been so focused on following my heart and my feelings that I don't listen to what the universe tries to tell me. My mom knew I was pregnant from the cards. She probably knew what was going to happen when we told Trey about Love, but everything is up to interpretation. Is it possible that this time is different?

"I don't know." I hang my head in shame, voicing my true feelings for the first time. "I'm scared."

"I know, hun, and it's alright to be afraid. But you can't let fear of the unknown stop you from seeing the beauty in the world." Bristol places her hand gently on my shoulder. "Go home. Take a bath. Relax. Hell, ask the cards again just to make sure you read them right the first time. But no matter what you do, you need to decide in your heart what's best for you. No one else can make you happy but you."

I look into my friend's eyes and see nothing but sympathy. Eager to get home and have some time to think, I ask, "Can you finish up by yourself?"

"Yes, now go home and take care of you. Vance and Selina will take care of Love." She wraps me in a tight hug before pushing my bag in my direction. Taking the hint, I grab it from the table and head home.

It isn't until I get home that I let myself think about my feelings for Connor. He's been genuine with me about his feelings, never avoiding telling me about his relationship with Lydia and how much she meant to him. Even though he still wore his wedding ring, I know it was more of a reminder of the love he was looking for. But he cast it all aside for me, to show me how much I mean to him. I've always been the one to love quickly and deeply, but my heart always ends up broken.

With Trey, it was my desire to fit in. The need to feel like I could be myself and still be accepted by those around me. Trey gave me that sense of being with a few kind words and a little bit of special attention. I would have done anything for him. All he had to do was ask. And ask, he did. I willingly gave him the most precious gift, and he threw it back in my face.

With Ian, I was careful. After being hurt so many times in the past, I guarded my heart. He was also kind to me, showered me with love and attention, worming his way into my heart. When I introduced him to Love, she was skeptical, but I believed it was because she didn't want to share me with someone else. She got on board after their second meeting, but I should've known then that something was wrong.

With both men, I was so desperate to be loved and accepted that I completely ignored how I felt when I was with them. In each relationship, I thought my feelings were the epitome of love, but they were nothing compared to my love for Connor.

As I climb the stairs and enter my room, I'm no closer to an answer, but my emotions seem to have calmed slightly. I know in my heart that I'm in love with Connor and that I need to find some way to make things right between us. But I also can't seem to silence the voice in the back of my head, whispering about all my insecurities and how one false move can ruin everything. Is it possible to make things any worse than they are right now? I don't think so. I can't go back to just being Connor's friend, someone he chats with when we happen to see each other.

To make matters worse, I've been using Love as my excuse. Love has always and will always be my number one priority, but my fear has cast a shadow over the life we are building here. Connor loves my daughter just as much as I love Jade. The four of us have slowly been growing closer to each other, but after what I said to him at the studio, I wouldn't be surprised if I ruined everything we were building. I was naïve to believe that I could stick my head in the sand and pretend none of this happened. I've been using my fear as an excuse to keep him at bay, but in the end, I ended up hurting all of us.

"Maybe a shower will help clear my head," I mumble as I walk into the bedroom. I gasp in surprise as my eyes lock on the tarot card sitting on my dresser. Every muscle in my body freezes as I lean forward, my eyes squinting slightly as I glance at the card, wanting to make sure I'm seeing it correctly.

"It's inverted." I gasp, covering my mouth with both hands, swinging my head back and forth as I try to process what I'm seeing.

If I were paying more attention to what the cards were saying earlier, I would have noticed that I had the meaning all wrong. The Devil card is a tricky one. When a tarot card is inverted, the meaning changes completely. My mom always said that when an inverted card shows up in your tarot reading, you have to listen to your gut to understand what it is telling you. It may be positive, negative, or neither—I just need to leave myself open to hear the lesson or message they are trying to tell me.

Bristol was right. I saw what I wanted to see. I was so focused on what could go wrong with our relationship that I closed myself off to the possibility that everything would work out in the end. By closing myself off to those possibilities, I was unable to see the message that the cards were trying to share with me. When I asked the cards if I was meant to be Lydia's replacement, pulling the Devil card would show that I was being trapped by her memory, leading me to believe that Connor never loved me. That I was only a placeholder for his dead wife until he tired of me or found someone better. So, I shut down, closing myself off from any other possibility.

But now, having had time to process and clear my mind, I get an entirely different reading of the card. With it being inverted, the Devil card means something entirely different. Connor isn't trying to replace his dead wife; he's finally ready to move on with me by his side.

"How could I have been so stupid?" I drop onto my bed, placing my head in my hands.

I try to run every scenario through my head, wanting to know exactly what I have to do to get Connor to forgive me, but I can't settle on the right one. My skin itches to grab my deck of cards and ask them what to do, but for the first time since I had Love, I want to make this decision myself. I don't want to base all my decisions on a deck of cards any longer. I could be way off base, crashing and burning epically, but at least I'll know I tried. Connor has done everything he can to break down the walls around my heart, drawing me gently out of my shell. I owe it to him—I owe it to us, to give a relationship a try. Giving my heart to Connor won't ruin our chances of finding a place to call home, but by opening my heart to him, it's possible for us to gain so much more.

My heart pounds in my chest, blood rushing through my ears. My vision blurs, as if I'm viewing the world through another lens. I'm panicking. I know it, and I'm powerless to stop my mind from running through all the ways things could go wrong if I don't get to Connor as quickly as possible.

"I have to go," I whisper into the room before running back down the stairs and out the front door.

The drive seems as if it takes forever, but it probably doesn't take longer than a few minutes before I see Connor's two-story Tudor home come into view. My hands are shaking as I turn off the car and climb out, racing toward the house.

Tears blur my vision as I rush toward the front door, wanting nothing more than to see Connor again and tell him how much I love him.

I come to a dead stop a few feet from the front door to catch my breath, my hands shaking as I reach for the door. Suddenly, it swings open, and I see Connor. A bright smile spreads across my face, eyes locked on him and taking in his every feature.

"I was wrong," I whisper before wrapping my arms around his neck, pulling him closer, and brushing my lips against his. "I love you."

eighteen

audrey

A feeling of home settles into my soul as I pour all my feelings into this kiss, hoping he will understand what he means to me. We break apart, gasping for air as Connor lifts me into his arms. "I thought I had lost you."

"Not lost, just took a small detour along the way." A mixture of fear and joy fills me as I worry I'm too late. His eyes snap to mine, scanning down my body before a blinding smile spreads across his face as he pulls me into his chest.

"I'm sorry, Connor."

"There's nothing for you to apologize for, beautiful." His arm snakes around my waist as he pulls me into the house, kicking the door shut.

I bury my nose in the side of his neck and inhale deeply, tears trickling down my face.

"What about the cards?"

"The cards had it right this time, not me. I was so terrified of getting my heart broken again that I let a silly deck of cards determine the outcome of my life. It was stupid."

"Audrey." Connor clenches his eyes shut tightly, pulling me closer to his chest.

I want to surrender to all the emotions inside me, but I need to make sure he understands why I did what I did. It was dumb, and it will never happen again, but I owe him an explanation.

"No. Don't talk. Just let me get all of this out." I take a deep breath, pulling back slightly so I can look into his eyes. "When my parents died, I was lost. I had just had a baby, not a full year beforehand, and had no other family to turn to. Thankfully, I had Bristol and her parents, but it wasn't the same. My mom had given me an old deck of tarot cards, and they became my guide. I asked them everything I could think of, feeling as if it was my mom guiding my life in the right direction."

A gut-wrenching sob escapes me as I bury my face in his neck. Snot and tears collect on his skin as I try to regain control of my emotions.

"At some point, instead of them being my guide, they became gospel. If the cards said something was a bad idea, then I didn't do it. I began to not trust myself to decide alone, having almost paralyzing anxiety about deciding anything without them."

Connor doesn't say a word as he rubs tiny circles on the bottom of my back, giving me the courage to continue.

"I was too afraid to take a chance on love. To allow my heart to guide me down the right path because all that has ever done is left me heartbroken and alone. But it wasn't the cards; it was me. I wanted so desperately to be loved by someone that I wasn't listening to what they had to say."

"How was this time different?" he asks, planting gentle kisses up my neck before pulling my ear between his teeth and biting down softly.

"Stop that." I moan as he releases my ear. "I can't focus when you do that."

"Sorry." He chuckles.

"Now, where was I?"

"You weren't listening to the cards."

"Right. So, I stopped listening to what the cards wanted to tell me. After everything that happened with Ian, I wanted to focus on Love and her well-being. I was tired of my bad decisions affecting her. I decided to swear off relationships, but then you came along and made me throw all my plans out the window."

I pull back slightly, resting my chin on his chest and staring into his eyes. "You're practically perfect. Everything I could ever want in a partner, but we've only known each other for a little over a month. I wondered if I could really jump into a relationship with you so soon. I was worried that I was making a mistake, so this morning, I went into my room and asked the cards if you were using me as a replacement for Lydia."

"Audrey, I would never—" he begins, but I interrupt him, slamming my eyes tightly closed so I don't see the pain in his eyes at my confession.

"I know you wouldn't, but I had to ask. To be sure that, this time, I wasn't making a mistake. But when I asked my question, I got the Devil card, which is basically the worst card possible when it comes to relationship readings. The minute I saw the card, my heart shattered into a million pieces. I wanted to be with you, to love you the way that I know you love me, but I was too afraid to take that leap without some confirmation from the cards. So, I pushed you away and tried to convince you that we couldn't be together."

"You're rambling." He chuckles, pulling me tightly to his chest and burying his nose into my neck.

"I know, but I do that when I'm nervous," I respond quickly, tightening my grip around his waist. "But I was wrong. The Devil card was inverted, which completely changed the answer to my question. You're not trying to replace me with Lydia. In fact, you are ready to move on with me by your side."

"That I am."

This is the moment of truth. No matter what the cards say, Connor is a human being with his own thoughts and feelings. He could decide that I'm not worth the hassle, that he'd rather quit before he got too involved, and he has every right to do so, but I'll never know unless I ask. I take a deep breath, slamming my eyes tightly shut and bracing for his response before I open my mouth and speak. "But I need to know if I'm too late or if there is a chance, even a small one, of us being together."

"I love you, Audrey Wilde. You aren't a replacement for Lydia. My feelings for you are more than I ever could've imagined them being in such a short amount of time."

"I know." I wrap my legs around his waist. "I love you, Connor."

He growls as he slams my back against the door. I grind my pussy into his cock, and it hardens. "Say it again," he whispers as he nibbles down the side of my neck.

"I love you." I moan as he presses his cock harder into my warm center, pinning me to the door. Connor looks into my eyes, searching for something. "I'm yours for as long as you'll have me."

"Forever," Connor grunts before his lips crash into mine again. I wrap my arms tighter around his neck, pulling myself into his chest, unable to get any closer. He slides his hand between our bodies, shoving my pants down and sliding his fingers between my folds. My gasp of surprise quickly turns into moans of pleasure as he pumps his fingers in and out of my pussy.

My hips rise off the door in time with his movements. I unwrap my arms from around his neck and reach for the button of his jeans. "I need you."

He pulls his fingers from my pussy and shoves them

into his mouth, licking them clean before placing my feet on the floor. “Turn around,” he commands, helping me turn to face the door and shoving my pants down around my ankles. He rubs his hand along my ass cheeks, giving them a hard smack before shoving his pants down to his ankles.

“I love you, Audrey,” he whispers into my ear before sheathing himself inside me. I rest my forearms on the door as Connor grips my hips tightly, pulling my ass back in time with each thrust.

“Oh, yes. Right there, don’t stop,” I beg as he continues to pound my pussy into submission.

He leans forward, resting his chest on my back before releasing one of my hips. Reaching between my legs, he grasps my clit between two fingers. “Come with me,” he whispers into my ear before squeezing my clit. We both come loudly, shouting each other’s name into the empty space.

We both hiss as Connor pulls out of me and bends down, pulling my pants and panties back over my hips. “I’m never letting you go.”

He plants a kiss on each of my eyelids, the tip of my nose, and my cheeks.

“Good, because I have no intention of letting you go either.” I snicker before he lifts me off the ground, molding his lips to mine. This kiss is everything, all our pain and love wrapped together in one.

We stand there for a few minutes, content with just being in each other’s embrace, when his phone chimes loudly in his pocket. He pulls it out and reads the screen. "That was Vance. He's bringing both girls here." My cheeks instantly pink, having completely forgotten about them.

"I asked Bristol to have him and Selina keep them company for a while."

"After I left Nurture Space, I asked him to pick up Jade from class and bring her home. I didn't expect you to come back."

"Well, I'm here now." I squeal as he lifts me into his arms and carries me into the living room. "I'm like a fungus. You're never getting rid of me."

"That would imply that I had planned on living without you." He gives me a bright smile before sitting down on the couch and placing me in his lap.

We are only able to enjoy the silence for a few moments before Vance's voice booms through the door. "Honey, we're home."

I attempt to slide off Connor's lap, but he pulls me back into his chest. "They better get used to seeing us together because I don't plan on ever letting you go."

"I like that plan," I respond with a smile as Vance, Selina, and the girls come piling into the room, asking a million questions at a time. The noise level quickly rises as the girls squeal in delight at seeing the two of us together.

"I know we asked for this, but can we keep the PDA to a minimum in the house?" Jade makes a gagging noise before plopping down on the couch beside us.

"We are sitting on the couch," I gripe.

"Yes, but it might take a little getting used to." Love wraps her arms around both of us, pulling us in for a quick hug.

"You owe us a hundred bucks." Jade points at Vance, holding out her hand.

"Why?" Connor asks as he places a kiss on both girls' cheeks. "Tell me you three didn't bet on whether Audrey and I would get together."

Vance chuckles. "We sure did. I owe them a hundred bucks, and Selina is going to go on a real date with me, thanks to this turn of events. I call that a win for me." Selina slaps him in the back of the head before heading right back out the door. "I'll leave you all to it. It's time to get my girl." He flashes us all a smile before following her out the door and closing it behind him.

"When are you guys moving in?" Jade questions lightly before Love asks, "Please don't make us share a room."

Connor and I look at each other and laugh. "Can we have dinner first? How does pizza sound?" The girls fist-pump the air before running into the kitchen to get a menu.

"Is this how our life is going to always be?" Connor asks as he leans toward me.

"No, it'll be better," I whisper before he captures my lips. We kiss for a few moments before we hear vomiting noises and break apart.

“We don’t want to see that!” both girls exclaim at the same time as they cover their eyes.

“You better get used to it,” Connor says before leaning in for another kiss. As I sink into his embrace, I realize the stars haven’t been against me. They’ve been leading me here to Connor. They took the long way around, but I have finally found my happily ever after.

nineteen

Vance

When I texted Selina asking to reschedule our dinner date, I expected her to give me a hard time, but nothing like this.

SELINA

No worries. I need to head home to pack. I got the call for my audition. Wish me luck.

VANCE

When do you leave?

My chest tightens as if all the air is being sucked out of the room and someone has wrapped their fingers around my neck. I struggle to take a breath as indescribable pain grabs hold of my heart and squeezes. I had plans to explain everything to her, to let her know that I was in this for the long haul, just like Connor and I talked about a few hours ago, but now I'm out of time.

SELINA

This afternoon. They need me back in New York tomorrow.

There are a million things I should be doing right now, but I can't move a muscle. It feels like all the air has been sucked out of the room as the grip around my heart tightens. I thought I'd have a chance to tell her everything I was too scared to say or ask for when we were younger. I was going to take a chance and put my heart on the line, lay everything at her feet, and hope she felt even a fraction of what I felt for her. But now, it's too late. Fuck. *Fuck*. She's going to leave me again without a second thought, but this time, I don't think I'll recover from my broken heart.

Right now, I can see what our lives could have been like if she'd chosen to stay with me. Not specifically here in Tyson's Creek, but with me. It never mattered where we were, as long as we were together. I'd have shown her how much I love, cherish, and care for her, every day until the end of time, but all of that is nothing but a dream. Selina is leaving me. Again. And I know I won't survive it.

My whole body shakes uncontrollably as tears pool in the corners of my eyes. I need to say something to let her know that this is tearing me apart, but will it even make a difference?

Searing pain flows through my entire body as waves of agony pull me under. I'm praying that I can hold on for just a little longer. Repeat to myself that the pain will subside at some point. It has to. I yearn for numbness to cut me off from all these feelings that I'm so desperate to forget. Beads of sweat dot my forehead as my eyes snap shut; my lips clamp tightly together as I fight to keep the screams of agony inside. I thought losing her the first time hurt, but this is beyond anything I could've imagined.

I push my fist into my eyes, trying to think of something—hell, anything, as the pain of losing Selina a second time tightens its hold around my heart, but this time, I fight it. I need to get a grip. Selina told me numerous times that she was leaving, that she had every intention to go back to New York, but I couldn't silence that part of me that hoped she'd stay here with me. That she'd choose to be with me. That to her, my love was enough.

"Hey, I think we're almost— What happened?" Connor grabs my shoulder, trying to get my attention.

"Selina is heading back to New York in a few hours." My voice cracks slightly as the tears I've been fighting to keep at bay stream freely down my cheeks.

"What? I thought..." His voice trails off, laced with confusion.

"Yeah, me, too." I chuckle not so humorously as I push to my feet and stride toward the door, flinging it open and heading directly to my truck.

I know there's nothing I can do to stop this. That rushing to the studio and begging her to stay or even let me go with her won't change anything between us. Selina is afraid of giving me that final piece of her heart, and if I push her to make a decision, I could lose her forever. She needs to understand what she means to me on her own. That I only want to be a part of her life, not force her to choose between what she loves and being with me. If I did that, I know she would crumble within herself, and it would be my fault.

Selina has always dreamed of being a ballerina. Asking her to stay and figure out whatever this is between us would be the end of us. She needs space to process everything that I've said to her and decide if being with me is enough, no matter where that might be. I need Selina to understand that I'd do anything for her, give her everything that I am, and all she has to do is give me her heart in return.

I angrily swipe at the tears streaming down my cheeks as I climb into my truck and drop my cell onto the seat beside me. My body is still shaking as I grip the steering wheel, trying to ground myself to do the one thing I know I need to do. I can't put off responding to her message. I want to find a way to tell her that this is tearing me apart, but I know it won't make a difference. I take a deep breath, reach for my phone with trembling hands, and do the same thing I've done for the last sixteen years.

I attempt to bear it.

VANCE

Okay. Good luck! I'd say break a leg, but that doesn't sound right. I know you'll do amazing. I love you.

And the moment I hit send, my heart shatters into a million pieces.

epilogue

connor

It's been almost a year since Audrey and Love moved to Tyson's Creek, bringing us to the girls' fifteenth birthdays. Of course, everyone knows these two aren't twins, but their birthdays are only a few weeks apart. Each girl had originally wanted their own celebrations, but when I told them what I had planned for the day, they gave in quickly. Audrey complained that she wanted both of them to feel special on their birthdays, but the girls reassured her that this was exactly what they wanted.

"A bit higher," Audrey directs me. She steps back before pronouncing the sign perfectly even. "Now you can start the grill. Everyone should be here in an hour or so."

"Where's my rifle?" I mumble, climbing down from the ladder. Audrey giggles as she wraps her arms around my neck.

"You're going to have to let them grow up. They aren't little girls anymore."

"Growing up is going to the movies alone or learning

to drive, not having boys come to my house while they are half-naked."

"Daddy! Calm down, you know everyone in this town. Do you honestly think anyone will do anything when you could just text their parents?" Jade whines as she comes bounding out of the back door and onto the deck.

I unwrap my arms from around Audrey and head to our outdoor kitchen to start the grill. I look out over the deck railing to the large in-ground pool the girls convinced me to put in when we built this house. We've only all been together here for a few months, but it feels like forever. Wanting to have a fresh start with Audrey, Vance and I built her dream house a few miles outside of town. Our craftsman-style house has a beautiful wrap-around porch, the perfect place for Love and Audrey to meditate and do yoga first thing in the morning.

"Don't worry, Dad. I'll keep an eye on her and make sure she doesn't get into any trouble." I turn and smile at Love as she brings me a large platter covered in hamburgers and hot dogs. Although a recent development, my heart swells each time I hear her call me *Dad*. Jade and I are still thick as thieves, but I've formed a special bond with Love. She's my daughter in almost every way possible, something that will be rectified as soon as she agrees to it.

I first brought up adopting Love with Audrey after we moved in. I wanted to make sure there was no doubt to anyone how much Love and her mother meant to me.

Audrey immediately agreed and we drafted up the paperwork, the only thing that we are waiting on is Love's approval.

I've been searching for the right time to bring up adoption with Love since we received the papers a few weeks ago, but it never felt right. Audrey also isn't in a hurry to get married, but I have other plans. Today seems like the perfect day to officially make us a real family. I reach into my pocket, gripping the black box nestled inside, holding the ring the girls and I had made for Audrey. "Is everything ready?" I ask Love in a hushed tone.

She has no idea about the adoption, but there was no way I was proposing to Audrey without including both our girls. After creating the perfect ring, the three of us came up with the perfect plan.

"The cards are sitting on the kitchen counter. There's no way my mom will resist reading our cards before the party." She gives me a quick thumbs-up before scurrying back inside.

I now have a better understanding of what the tarot cards mean to Audrey. Shortly after she and Love moved in with us at our old house, Audrey explained to me about reading tarot cards and has even started doing readings for Jade and some of our friends. It's no longer about using the cards to avoid making decisions, but as a way of helping the people she loves have a better understanding of why they make the decisions they do. I still don't understand everything, but if a card helped her discover we were meant to be together, maybe the card could help me find the right moment to propose.

As if on cue, Jade and Audrey come barreling out the door and take a seat at the table. "Mom, you need to read Dad's cards," Jade whines, causing Audrey to smile softly.

Jade calling Audrey *Mom* has been happening almost since we officially got together. Audrey was worried the first time that it happened, fearing that I'd somehow view it as her trying to make Jade forget about her mother, but that was never the case. Jade told her that she would always love and care for the woman who gave her life, but she believed Lydia wouldn't mind allowing Audrey to have the title of Mom, and I wholeheartedly agreed.

"I need to know if I should warn Mason. He might kill him." Jade winks at me over Audrey's shoulder.

I try to cover my growl with a cough at the mention of Mason's name. The last thing any father wants to hear about is the punk-nose kid who has his sights set on his daughter.

"He wouldn't kill him," Audrey responds matter of factly before wrapping her arms around my waist. "None of us want him to go to jail."

"Who are we killing?" Vance asks before slapping me on the back. "It's only murder if we get caught." We both laugh loudly right as the door bursts open again as Bristol's almost one-year-old daughter, Rebekah, comes waddling out the door, followed closely by her mother.

Bristol is hunched over, waddling along like a duck with both of her hands outstretched on either side of

Rebekah. Every time the little one starts to lean one way or the other, Bristol is right there to catch her, holding her tightly as Rebekah regains her balance before she takes off again.

"Sorry, little one, but I have a feeling Mommy's back needs a break," Vance says as he scoops Rebekah up into his arms and plants a kiss on her forehead.

"Thank you." Bristol groans as she stands up straight, gripping her lower back in her hands. "Does it get any easier?"

"Nope. You just stop worrying so much about them falling and hurting themselves. It's a fact of life and is bound to happen."

"Says the guy that fastened pillows to the front and back of Jade's body when she was learning to walk because you were afraid of her getting hurt." Vance chuckles as I grab Rebekah from his arms.

"Shut up. No one asked you," I retort, causing everyone to laugh loudly.

I leave Vance to man the grill and head over to all the ladies sitting at the table. Stepping up behind Audrey, I lean down and plant a kiss on her cheek. "What do the cards say is in store for us today?"

Audrey gives me a quizzical look before pointing down at the cards. "Since you weren't available, I told Jade I would read my own. I asked what my future holds, but the cards' response is puzzling."

I look at Love, and she smiles brightly, wrapping her arms around Jade. Tears fill both their eyes as they jump up and down slightly. "Tell him what they say, Mom," Love whispers.

Audrey points at the top card and begins explaining. "This card is the Hierophant card. It represents tradition. The next card is the Justice card, which makes sense if I have to bail you out of jail tonight, but this last card confuses me." Her hand moves over to the third card, pointing to what seems to be a man and woman holding cups and facing each other. There is a face with wings drawn above them, as if it's presiding over a ceremony. "This card is the Two of Cups, which symbolizes commitment."

I chuckle in response, understanding the meaning of the cards quickly. "Well, if the cards say it's time..." I motion for Bristol to come get Rebekah before handing her to her and I stride around the table toward Love, her eyebrows pull down in confusion, trying to make sense of what is happening.

"Aren't you supposed to be proposing to my mom?" Love says as Jade unwraps her arms from around her.

"I'll get to that, but I need to ask you a question first," I respond with a smile as I reach into my pocket.

"Couldn't this have waited, Daddy?" Jade replies, crossing her arms over her chest.

"No. I've waited long enough to tell the world that Love is my daughter just as much as you. Been looking for the perfect time to bring it up, and now seems like as good of a time as any."

"What?" Love whispers as she pushes back from the

table and stands in front of me, her entire body shaking with emotion.

"I want to adopt you, Love. I don't need a piece of paper to know you're my little girl, but I figured it was time to make it official."

Everyone gasps in shock as Love throws her arms around me, squeezing me tightly. "Yes," she croaks, burying her nose in my chest as I lock eyes with Audrey over her head. Tears are streaming down her cheeks as she pushes back from the table and runs toward us. I open my arms and pull Jade into our embrace as Audrey hugs me from behind. The four of us stay like that for a few moments before we break apart with a laugh.

"Is it my turn now?" Audrey sniffles as she wipes the tears from her cheeks, a blinding smile on her face.

"It sure is," I respond before turning around and dropping to one knee, pulling the black box from my pocket. "Fate has brought us together, whether it be your deck of tarot cards or a higher power. I will love you and our daughters for the rest of my life. Will you marry me?"

Audrey's hands fly to her mouth as tears fall from her eyes. "Yes!" she screeches so loudly that my ears ring before she throws herself at me, toppling us both down onto the deck. Cheers erupt from around us as I bring her in for a passionate kiss.

Audrey always believed the stars were against us, but if this moment proves anything, it's that our love was written in the stars.

I hope you enjoyed Before I Love You! Wondering what happened to Connor, Audrey, Jade and Love after the end? Scan the QR code for instant access to a bonus epilogue for your new favorite couple.

Already subscribed? Just check your last newsletter for the link to my bonus material! If you can't find it, you can simply resubscribe and the scene will be yours in minutes!

USA Today Bestselling Author AJ Alexander has been writing romance since 2018. She loves writing small town romances with found families and all the nosey nellies that help her characters find their happily ever afters! She lives in Arizona, otherwise known as the surface of the sun, with her husband, two daughters, two cats, and a lovable golden retriever.

When she isn't writing you can find AJ reading, binging the latest true crime documentary on Netflix, or binging the latest Korean Drama or Anime that's released. AJ is a cynical hopeless romantic that believes in love at first sight, that bigger is always better, and everything should be put off for a nap.

Come find her in the wild! There's nothing she loves more than connecting with my readers.

www.ingramcontent.com/pod-product-compliance
Lightning Source LLC
LaVergne TN
LVHW100518110826
845146LV00002B/691

* 9 7 9 8 9 8 9 8 2 5 0 0 4 *